Issue 9 Autumn 2017

Science fiction magazine from Scotland

ISSN 2059-2590
ISBN 978-1-9997002-3-2

Shoreline of Infinity is available in digital or print editions.
Submissions of fiction, art, reviews, poetry, non-fiction are welcomed:
visit the website to find out how to submit.

www.shorelineofinfinity.com

Publisher
Shoreline of Infinity Publications / The New Curiosity Shop
Edinburgh
Scotland

110917

Contents

We are grateful to **Martyn Turner**, who sponsored the artwork for *Spirejack* in this issue. Martyn has supported us on Patreon for almost a year now and we thank him for his generosity. For more information on sponsorship please visit our Patreon site at www.patreon.com/shorelineofinfinity

Cover: **Reader at the Thought Discharger**
Stephen Pickering

Editorial Team
Editor & Editor-in-Chief:
Noel Chidwick

Art Director:
Mark Toner

Deputy Editor & Poetry Editor:
Russell Jones

Reviews Editor:
Iain Maloney

Assistant Editor & First Reader:
Monica Burns

Copy editors:
Iain Maloney, Russell Jones, Monica Burns

Extra thanks to:
Caroline Grebbell, M Luke McDonell, Katy Lennon, Abbie Waters

First Contact
www.shorelineofinfinity.com
contact@shorelineofInfinity.com
Twitter: @shoreinf
and on Facebook

Pull Up a Log

"What science fiction writers can do is to inspire and to warn"
—Cory Doctorow, p104

Shoreline of Infinity spent a lot of time this summer at the Edinburgh International Book Festival – handily on our doorstep. We were honoured to be asked to host our live science fiction cabaret Event Horizon, and also to publish a special edition of Shoreline of Infinity, Issue 8½. This gave us a good excuse to include contributions from writers Ken MacLeod invited to talk at the Festival, as well as stories from Scottish writers we published in *Shoreline of Infinity*. Take a peek at the back cover ad to see what a fine line-up we had.

Our contributors took the chance to reflect on the role of science fiction in this topsy-turvy world. Ken MacLeod in his guest editorial says "SF can't predict the future, but it can shape it" and "we read it for entertainment and enlightenment."

Charles Stross points out that "what we write reflects the zeitgeist, so when current affairs seem menacing our visions of the future turn dark and dismal" but noting the time lag between conception and publication. Iain Maloney backs up Stross's thoughts with the observation of the domination of dystopia in young adult fiction, and shows how Scotland is more than pulling its weight in "producing its fair share of near-future dystopias."

And in this issue of *Shoreline of Infinity*, Cory Doctorow adds: "But I think what science fiction writers can do is to inspire and to warn – we can help people think about different ways of approaching the problems that are coming."

So when someone asks you why you read – or write – science fiction, you can tell them it's the most important thing you can do.

No pressure, folks, but by reading this issue of *Shoreline* you are helping to save the world – and having some fun along the way.

Noel Chidwick
Editor-in-Chief
Shoreline of Infinity
September 2017

The Last Days of the

Lotus Eaters

Leigh Harlen

Art: P Emerson Williams

The earth, and the creatures in it ate her flesh, but the tree kept her bones, its roots wrapped around and entwined every remaining bit of her. Wind stirred the branches of the tree and it tickled as if it were her own leaves being caressed and tossed about. Birds perched on the branches and she felt their hopping feet and heard the chirps of their offspring. She remembered what it was to have a beating heart, breath in her lungs, and feel the wind toss her hair about, so that it tickled her face. She was awake, but not alive.

Lita wasn't forgotten immediately. After she was buried, when she was only half awake, the roots not yet able to reach her bones, she heard her parents weep above her. Every day they came to wail and lament and she hated them. Hated them for not believing her. When her flesh was consumed and the roots fused to her bones huge blossoms appeared on the tree that for years had produced fewer and more pitiful flowers as it died little by little. Now they were rich and fragrant, dense and beautiful in a way she had heard the old folks talk about when they were melancholy and nostalgic and flushed with too much wine.

Her parents gasped, taking the blossoming to be a sign, a comfort. She felt the tug as they each plucked one, the grinding of their teeth as they chewed, reveling in its sweetness. The flowers slid down their throats, into their acid filled bellies and then plucked out their memories, their fear, and their grief. It all passed into her, tasting like bitter dust. Her mother's agony as she was birthed, and her father's joy mixed with terror as he held her tiny body in his arms for the first time, thinking how fragile she was and how much his life was about to change. She saw herself running through the woods and understood the fear they had shoved down brought on by her careless certainty that no matter where she ran or how high she jumped she would never be hurt. And she felt the doubt that had crept in when she told them over and over that the sky shouldn't be so black, so empty, and there should be life beyond the walls of their little village. Their minds were emptied of all that made them doubtful and unhappy while she felt swollen and sick.

At night, the wind stirred the blossoms and carried pollen through the air and into the lungs of the sleeping villagers, dulling the fears that had been growing as the tree died. When people heard that it was producing flowers again, they came to eat them and one by one their fears and doubts were erased completely and buried in her.

Only the priests took vows not to eat the flowers, though they were also soothed by its pollen, their faith fortified and guilt dulled if not erased. They read secret texts that told them what to do to keep the tree from dying and they needed to remember. All except one, one priest was given leave to break his vows and eat the blossoms. The one who had killed her.

He walked up to the tree and picked a flower. With his other hand he took out a flask and raised it to the tree. "I truly am sorry, Lita, you were a remarkable young woman. But you were wrong." He took a sip of wine and ate the flower and gave her his memories.

The night he heard that there was a little girl who talked about stars and the end of the universe, he was relieved and terrified. The tree was dying and they needed to revive it, but he had hoped that necessity would come when he had passed his position on to a younger priest. He stayed awake all night, reading the holy book to fortify his nerves and staring into the flickering light of a candle knowing it would still be years before the ritual could be performed, the text and his conscience demanded certainty.

In the bright morning she was running through the grass, running so fast she felt like maybe she could outrun the end of the world. She stopped when he stood in front of her.

"Lita, could I walk with you for a little while?" he said.

7

She had been taught to trust and respect the priests and though she wanted to keep running, she nodded.

"I heard you telling stories at the market yesterday," he said.

"They aren't stories. The night sky is empty and it didn't used to be. I read about stars in the library, there were so many of them and they were so beautiful that people wrote poetry about them and used them to navigate. There was a moon and there were huge oceans. Entire planets where people lived and travelled. Not just one little village with an empty sky," she said.

He smiled. "Most people would say those are just stories, fairy tales. It's unusual for a girl your age to believe such things."

She glared at him. "They aren't made up. Why would so many of the ancient writers all make-up something like that?" She wouldn't be reasoned with, not about this. She had told her parents, her grandparents, her friends and their parents since she was old enough to look at the sky and wonder why there was nothing but the sun in all that big black emptiness. No one believed her, she had hoped the priest would be different, that he would know some arcane secrets and share them with her.

Having consumed those secrets, she understood he was different, he did know. He had wanted her to say, "Yes, you're right. They're just stories." He wanted her to take it all back because he liked her, he liked that she was smart and not afraid to argue with him. He didn't want to have to kill her, but there was also a coldness in him, a small shard at the center that made him certain that he could, that gave him a feeling of righteousness. He was doing what was best for everyone. What was one little girl's life in the face of chaos and despair for an entire people?

He left her alone with her confusion but he didn't leave her completely. She often saw him out of the corner of her eye, listening to her conversations just a little too intently, watching her when the villagers gathered to dine together with a dark and contemplative expression.

A couple of years after that first strange conversation, he stopped her while she was walking home from school.

"Would it be alright if I walked with you?" he said.

"Of course." Even if he was a bit strange, her parents would send her to bed without dinner if she was rude to a priest.

"Tell me, do you still think the sky is too empty?" he said.

"I know it is."

"What if you're right? What would be the purpose of knowing?"

Lita hadn't thought about that. She'd spent her life so angry and frustrated that no one believed her that she hadn't thought much about why she wanted so badly for them to know beyond simple vindication.

"The sun is a star. Whatever happened to the stars could happen to our sun too and we'd all die."

"And what would you do about it?"

"I-I don't know. I just think people should know."

"Would it make them happier to know if there's nothing to be done about it? What would be the point of being good, of having children, working for a future that might be snuffed out with the sun at any moment?" he said.

She frowned. "Why would knowing the truth mean people don't do those things?"

"Does that belief make you happier? Because it seems to me you don't have any interest in those things. You don't have many friends and you've never expressed interest in having a boyfriend or a girlfriend like other girls your age. Your teachers say you've never talked about wanting to be a farmer, a builder, a healer, a baker, or any other role in the village when you finish your studies. Do you see yourself having a future?"

She wasn't unhappy, but it was true that she took little interest in planning for the future and her insistence that the world had ended and they were the last to know drove people away and gave her a reputation for being strange.

"I don't object to doing those things, they just don't seem very important," she said.

"I think you are quite remarkable in that. Most people who believed that would lose all hope, they would do nothing but wallow in their despair and possibly act out in rage and be violent to others or themselves. But even if everyone took the knowledge

9

as well as you but the sun was still there and shining bright for fifty years, a hundred years, we would still need to plan for a future. We would still need food and people to heal us when we're sick or hurt. We would still be better for having lived full lives."

"Are you trying to tell me that I should stop telling the truth?"

"I am asking you to consider that maybe other people should not know it."

"But they're believing a lie, it's not right. I don't know how to explain why it's not right, but it's not."

The priest sighed. She understood now that he was seeking some kind of acceptance or consent from her to do what he knew must be done to sooth his own conscience. But at the time she had been confused, he was talking to her as if he might believe her but it gave her no peace because he was raising questions she didn't have answers to and making her feel foolish. It was evident to her that it was true and people should know it for the very simple reason that it was wrong not to know the truth.

The priest came to her one more time shortly before she was to finish her schooling. She was sitting in the grass reading from a dusty book she had found in the library, a book about cosmology and theories about the creation of the universe. It had been filed as science fiction and forgotten by everyone but her.

"I hear you've decided to become a teacher, Lita," he said.

She nodded. Although the priest made her uncomfortable, she was also happy to see him. In her sixteen years, he was the only person who had ever engaged with her about her belief that the universe was ending, even though she left each conversation feeling confused and chastised, it was a relief to be taken seriously and she felt more prepared to argue with him each time.

"Would you care to walk with me a bit?" he said.

She closed her book and slipped it into her bag. "Okay."

"What led you to want to teach?"

"There are so many things we've forgotten. Technology that could make our lives easier and maybe even save us if someone with a brain that works just the right way learns about it."

"You still think the world is ending?"

"I know the universe is ending. Everything is being pulled further and further apart and soon it's going to start getting too cold to grow things, then it will get too cold to live on the surface and we'll need to go underground, and eventually it will be too cold to live anywhere. We need to prepare."

"That doesn't sound like something anyone could prepare for. If annihilation is inevitable, why not let people live happily until the end?" he said.

"Maybe it is inevitable. But we would last longer and we might have a chance to avoid it for a long time if only people knew. And I think that's worth the fear and even the despair."

They came to the dying tree and he stopped and looked at her. "You are very certain of yourself."

She was proud, for the first time she felt she came out of a conversation with the priest as the victor. "I am."

He pulled a small flask from his jacket. "I still disagree. I think you are young and idealistic and want to believe that people think and act like you, that they would accept inevitable doom with grace and resilience. But I do admire you."

"Thank you," she said.

He raised the flask. "To the moral certainty of youth and to the intellect and tenacity you have grown into so

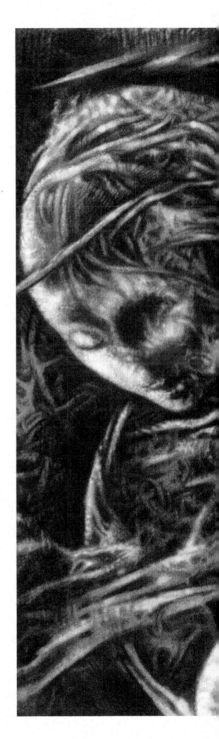

well." He took a drink – although she now knew that he let it graze his lips and slosh back inside.

He passed the flask to her. "Just a sip, I can't have it said a holy man is getting young women drunk." She hesitated, but she was flattered and her parents only let her have wine on holy days. She took a sip. It tasted like vinegar and ash and in just seconds she was unconscious.

The priest believed that the drug would prevent her from waking up and feeling any part of the ritual, but he was wrong. The tree did not share the priest's minimal compassion and the ritual was not one that it allowed its sacrifice to sleep through. She also knew from being forced to carry his memories that even if he had known, he would have buried her still alive at the base of the tree anyway, such was his faith and conviction.

When she woke, she choked on the dirt and screamed as the roots bore into her like hungry fingers, ripping into her soft skin, ravenous for the life bleeding out of her body and the taste of the knowledge that had marked her for death. It had been a long time since it had been given a new life to nourish it.

As the blossom pulled out and transferred the priest's memories of her and of how he had liked her and how he had vomited when he heard her muffled screams coming up through the ground, she wanted to tell him that she still knew he was wrong and that she still intended to be a teacher in her own way.

He walked away, his mouth still sweet from the blossom he had consumed and his mind emptied of terrible memories and doubts about the righteousness of his actions. He returned to the priesthood a blank slate, prepared to watch for the next girl who wanted to know why the sky was so dark.

Years passed and her parents and all the people she had known when she was alive died, their names soon as forgotten as her own to the handful who struggled to survive on the increasingly hostile surface. The sun still shone in the sky, but it looked smaller, the plants began dying, and the people above whispered through frostbitten fingers, "Winter is almost over, summer is on its way." But she knew winter would never end and soon the people above forgot that there had been such a thing as summer.

The tree alone stayed green and every night it spread pollen on the wind so that they could believe winter was all there was and they shouldn't look too hard at the sky. As her bones crumbled, the blossoms began to shrink and there were less and less of them each year so the people saved eating them only for holy days and slowly their doubts began to grow.

A young girl came and sat at the base of the tree.

"I don't have any friends. They all think I'm strange. Yesterday a group of big kids tried to throw me in the river because I told them winter didn't used to last forever. It used to get warm and green. I read it in a book. A little kid was swinging on a rope and they jumped into a lake and didn't get sick and have to be warmed up afterwards. They picked flowers, not like from you where we eat them, but just because there were so many and they were pretty. I wish you weren't just a tree so you could talk to me." The girl stood and ran away.

Soon after, the girl's teacher came to eat the blossoms and she swallowed his doubts and the fear he felt when a priest came and asked about her, wanting to know what she wrote about in her school essays and if she had any plans for the future.

The possibility of a future was almost gone. Soon it would be too cold for anyone to survive on the surface and they would need to go underground and start learning the tools to extend their survival as long as possible. And just like she had known, that little girl would be certain that people deserved to know and that immunity to the lie marked her for death because there were no words to convince a zealous and righteous priest that she was right. She couldn't save her own life and she couldn't return the possibility that knowledge gave to the rest of the village, only the tree could do that.

She didn't have much time if any knowledge returned to the village was to be of any help, but she would have to wait until the girl was a little older, old enough to read and understand more than just children's stories.

The new priest came to the girl again. The tree was dying fast and he didn't wait as long between conversations as the old priest had for Lita.

The girl came to sit at the base of the tree as had become her custom.

"I wish I knew how to explain to the priest that it's important for people to know the truth, I felt stupid. It's just so obvious, it doesn't make sense why I'm the only who sees it. You're starting to die, but you're still green and nothing else is, it's not normal, I don't care how 'spiritually important' a tree is, it can't survive the cold so well," the girl said.

Lita felt hope for the first time since she died. She reached out, one of the branches flicked and the backpack she had been carrying the day the priest had buried her slipped from the hole where it had fallen unnoticed.

The girl picked it up and opened it. One by one took the books out and flipped through the pages.

"Did you do that?" She looked amazed and suspicious but she sat at the base of the tree and read for hours. When night descended she put the books back in the bag and ran home.

Even though they did not affect her, the girl stopped eating the blossoms on holy days so Lita had no idea what the girl might have figured out from the books or about who they had belonged to.

One night, under cover of darkness, the girl came out to the tree with a ladder and one by one, plucked off each blossom and burned them in a pile.

There was terror and outrage in the village the next day when they discovered all of the flowers were gone, although no one knew who had done it. It was an ingenious idea, and Lita was delighted by the girl's cleverness, but the blossoms grew back. During the weeks it took however, questions and doubts flourished in the little village.

The girl's parents came to the tree and prayed. They ate two of the small blossoms even though they knew it was forbidden outside holy days to preserve the few remaining. They were deeply troubled by their daughter's insistence that the tree was somehow blinding everyone to the fact that the world was ending, that the sky shouldn't be empty, and the sun used to be nearer. And they were growing distrustful of the priest who came and asked them about her, if she told them her theories and if they thought she believed what she said or if she was just a girl telling stories.

That night, the girl came one more time. She opened a bottle of alcohol and poured it on the tree and set it ablaze.

In the ground, Lita screamed silently, not since the tree had ripped her apart had she felt pain like that. She thrashed and the tree above shook and groaned. People ran from the village and threw buckets of water on it.

It smoldered for days, but the fire did not kill the tree, not completely, she wasn't sure if the tree could be killed. But it was badly hurt and would not be able to grow blossoms for a long time. Desperate for nourishment to heal itself, it gripped her fragile bones in its roots as if it were wringing the last drops of water out of a sponge. It squeezed until her bones turned to dust and the memories and knowledge she had swallowed for so many years soaked the earth. With no other soul to carry that burden, the hungry roots drank in all of the secrets she had kept for so long.

After several months, the tree began to regrow and a few pitiful, tiny flowers bloomed, still fueled by the last bits of Lita's life it had stored in its roots. That night, when the wind blew it carried pollen laced with generations of knowledge and memories, dusting the sleeping survivors with doubt and questions.

The next morning, the girl awoke to a village gripped with chaos and panic. She looked at the tree, blackened and skeletal, looming on the hill over the village and whispered a thank you.

Leigh Harlen is a speculative fiction writer who lives in Seattle with their partner and an adopted family of rats and rabbits. Their work has been published in *Aurealis, Turn to Ash,* and *Dark Moon Digest.* Follow them on Twitter @leighharlen for updates on future publications.

Keeping the Peace

Catriona Butler
& Rob Butler

Narla sees Zola climbing a tree in the blazing summer sunshine. Her brother's skin gleams with a deep brown tan. He doesn't need to worry about skin cancer. He's laughing. He knows he can't fall – at least, not this year.

Reluctantly she withdraws her gaze from the windows and tunes in again to the droning of her schoolteacher. Narla is in the Female 80+ stream so she has to concentrate on job skills, childbirth, caring for elderly relatives and, finally, the demands required for her own, inevitable senility. All in that order. Her whole life is very orderly.

Unlike Zola's.

Haenna's hands close over Narla's tightly clenched fists. Their eyes meet.

"Try not to think about it, Narla. I know it's so hard but he's still got at least six months and look how he's enjoying himself."

Narla puts on her grateful face, whispers 'thank you' to her friend and deliberately relaxes her fingers. Haenna smiles at her and pats her shoulder.

They resume their studies but Narla's eyes are soon drawn back to the window and the sight of Zola now hanging upside down from the top branches. *Yes, she thinks, look at him enjoying himself. That's all he ever does. The government actually pays him to have fun, and all because he's going to die when he's 13. But me, I'm going to live to be 82. Whoopee. So I have to go to school all day while he just enjoys himself.*

Six months later, Narla stirs her porridge while Zola toys with his fried breakfast. He normally wolfs it down but today is his 13th birthday. She glances at her father, pretending he's reading the newspaper, and her mother biting her lip as she makes sandwiches. Zola leaps up, breakfast abandoned, grabs his lunch and stuffs it into a bag.

"I'm going out to play."

"Be careful, dear". Their mother puts her hands to her mouth. She's never had to say that before. She reaches out to clutch him but Zola squirms away.

"I'm sorry, Zola, but you must be careful now. You could still have a full year, you know."

"I know," he snarls and is gone.

His mother watches him with an aching gaze through the frosty window. All that snow. Narla imagines her mother thinking of him sliding on ice and crashing over onto his head.

She tries to stop herself smiling.

"Can I have his bacon and eggs?"

"Of course not, darling. You know it's bad for you."

Narla slams down her spoon. "Hello. I'm going to live to 82. How can something be bad for me? It makes no sense."

"Not this again, Narla," snaps her father, "not today please. You know full well that you need to keep healthy so you won't spend a large part of your long life ill or in hospital. That's not really what you want is it? Let's just try and think about poor Zola today can we?"

Of course, she thinks bitterly. *Poor Zola.*

After a few minutes of tense silence her father clears his throat.

"There is, at least, some good news in the paper today."

"What's that, dear?"

"A new sentient has been born and her life prediction is 95."

"Oh, how wonderful."

"It's a pity these sentients don't just die out," muttered Narla, still wondering if she could nick a bit of bacon without anybody seeing her.

Her father lowers his paper. "Narla. How can you say such a thing? What is the matter with you today?"

Narla shrugs.

"I just think we might be better off without them, that's all."

Her father sighs.

"Better off without them? Can you imagine what that would be like? Nobody would know when they were going to die. We wouldn't be able to plan for anything. Life would be chaotic."

"Well, it used to be like that," grumbled Narla, "we learnt all about it in History class."

"Then you should also have learned how the sentients have brought peace and certainty to the world. There are no more wars, no more suffering..."

"What about those terrorists on the news who know they can't be killed?"

"They are being dealt with by the authorities..."

"And all those rumours about some of the sentients being frauds?"

"Hearsay and tittle-tattle. Listen to me, Narla. The sentients are our salvation. The more that are born, the more information we can gather about the future, and the better it will be for everybody. We know how long we will live and our expectations and ambitions are adjusted

18

accordingly. Without this knowledge poor Zola would not have had such a happy, carefree childhood."

"No, he'd have been at school all the time, like me. It's not fair. Why can't I have some fun as well?"

"Narla. That's a terrible thing to say."

A year later and it's approaching midnight. The family sit quietly in their lounge. Zola is trembling. His mother hugs him to her.

He whispers. "There's only ten minutes left. How's it going to happen? I feel fine. It must be some explosion or accident or something." He leaps up. "I should get away from you. Whatever it is could kill all of you as well."

Narla sniggers. "Don't be stupid. I'm going to live to 82, Dad's going to live to 78, Mum's..."

"Narla, please!"

"Well, I'm just saying."

"Well don't."

Silence.

A knock on the door.

The adults glance anxiously at each other. Narla's father crosses to the window, pulls aside the curtain by an inch or two and looks out.

"Who is it, dear?"

He slowly closes the curtain but does not turn to face them. He seems to sag.

"Armed police. Dozens of them. All around the house."

Catriona has previously been a joint author on some research papers but this is her first fiction publication. **Rob** has had short stories published in a number of places including Shoreline of Infinity 5. In this first writing collaboration between daughter and father there were remarkably few arguments!

Death Acceptance

Tony Clavelli

Art: Jessica Good

The phone rings and though it's early, I'm hoping someone has died. Anything other than Richard calling again would be fine.

"Full Lives Funerary Directing, this is Gina," I say.

"Hello," a woman says. "I've got a human body I'd like for you to transport." Her voice is calm and crisp even at this hour.

"Okay, can you please tell me the name and address of the deceased?" I say, before I recognize that no nursing home caregiver would specify that it was a *human* body.

"I have all of the paperwork from the coroner, so this is all perfectly normal."

I cough. This is either hilarious or terrifying. The unwavering cordiality and gentleness of a funeral director is a fine-honed skill. And I'm good at it.

"Of course it is," I say. "And the name, again?"

"Her name is Red Posy," she says. I get an address and then she hangs up.

I call up my assistant Kathleen and I hear her burr grinder buzzing. I hired her not because she's a particularly great embalmer, but because she's so damn prompt. She can put on a clean suit and sympathetic smile at superhuman speeds. Having a warm face at the front of the home at a moment's notice goes a lot further than masking the death pallor under inches of powder.

I shower and eat some dry toast, and by the time I'm downstairs, Kathleen is already waiting for me in the garage. She hands me a travel mug of black coffee and gets in the passenger seat of the transport coach. The coach is new so the AutoDrive is competent enough that I can keep both hands on the mug and watch the sun creep up between the trees.

"Did the caller give any specifics about our totally-normal-human, other than that her name is a bundle of flowers?" Kathleen asks. She uses the visor mirror to check her makeup.

"A caller of intrigue," I say. Then I remember Kathleen is still trying to learn as much as she can. "Probably just in a shock. Folks say weird things around the dead."

"Right turn," the dash announces, and then the car slows and turns down a narrow tree-lined road.

"Oh my god," Kathleen says. She claps her hands together and laughs. "That explains everything."

"What? You know this street?"

"This is a *borg* neighborhood," she says, and I wince at the word. In my business it is essential to maintain an impeccable level of correctness, even for NextState people. Though some get a kick out of being called a replicant, you just don't say "borg." It's not even accurate – they're not biological at all.

"Oh, come on," she says. "You can't say they don't give you creeps."

"No," I say. "You can't say that they do."

"Of course I wouldn't in front of customers. But they're suspicious."

"Kathleen. When we get up there – "

"Can't trust 'em. They're taking over, you know." She sees me reach for the manual brakes. "Okay, sorry! I'm done." She checks herself in the mirror again, flashes that smile to herself, and then presents it to me. I roll my eyes, but it is reassuring.

The driveways stretch so far that the enormous houses set back in the trees are barely visible from the street. Through the leaves, I can make out the uniformly large, gray buildings, three story cement cubes with dozens of narrow windows. The landscaping leading up to them is gorgeously kept.

We pass five or six of these before the car slows again, and the dash says, "Arriving at destination."

The coach rolls backwards down the drive and stops at a sidewalk to the front door. Bright white tulips poke through the purples of phlox and rockcress that line the stone-edged garden. I hated flowers as a kid, always corpse-side and rotting faster than the bodies. I'd never have imagined the NS were into flowers. The door opens for us before we get a chance to ring.

Hiding halfway behind the door is an NS, a woman, with a beautiful blood-red finish. Older models attempted to look perfectly human but never quite crossed the uncanny valley (a common accusation directed at morticians, though fortunately not at me). Now they don't bother to appear human. This one has hundreds of wires sprouting neatly from the top of the head and falling down behind her, positioned to look like hair the same color as the skin. The one eye visible from the doorframe looks more like the digital lens that it is rather than a human eye. It scans us.

"Hello. We're Full Lives," Kathleen says. She's wearing that soft, sincere smile that doesn't look too happy or too sad. "We can roll a gurney around, or...?"

"That is kind but not really necessary," the NS woman says. I recognize her voice from the phone call earlier. "I'll be out." She closes the door on us then. We walk back to the coach.

"This is super weird," Kathleen mutters.

"Yeah," I say.

"I guess I just assumed that people never come to these places," she says, and then catches herself. "I mean, you know, people like us."

She means the kind of people who tend to die.

Soon the same NS woman we had talked to before comes out. She wears a thin black dress that presses against her in the morning breeze, showing the contours of her humanoid body. She moves with perfect fluidity but with a slight slouch to her gait – she must have been an expensive build. She hands me a manila folder.

"It's all there," she says. "Death certificate, coroner's letter."

"Do you need help with Ms. Posy's body?" Kathleen offers, though the crinkle in her nose suggests that she's coming to the same conclusion that I am.

"I'm Red Posy," she says. I look at the papers and see all of the standard stuff, except the references – beside the cause of death and the coroner's stamp on the bottom are notes about Article 81G, handwritten and then stamped over. As I'm puzzling through these, Red climbs into the open trunk of my coach.

"Hey, um," Kathleen says but then gives up.

"Can we please leave?" Red asks. "You can see there that I've died and it's legal. I know I said I was human over the phone, but it is my legal right to do so."

Kathleen already has that eight-teeth smile on as she leans into the trunk. Red sits with her legs stretched out beside the gurney, her steel-shoed feet surprisingly dainty. Her eyes – the glowing sclera and cobalt iris so starkly contrasted against the red of her skin – look impossibly alive. Nothing like the digital cameras I thought I saw in them before. With a turn of her wrist, Red holds out her palm to Kathleen.

"Have you conversed through an NS before?" she asks Kathleen.

"No," Kathleen says.

"Just talk into the palm. The sound comes out the tips of the fingers."

Red cups Kathleen's face with her hand and Kathleen jerks away at first, and then eases back.

"Oh my god, it's ringing," Kathleen says. Red lets out a frustrated sigh.

The call is to Red's lawyer, who unfortunately is Richard Polymore. Richard was my boyfriend for about eight months, and though he hadn't done any work with NS rights in the past, he's now assisting Red Posy to exercise her rights to a comfortable death.

Kathleen is relaying all this to me when she asks, "Can we just put him on speaker?"

"No," I say, but Red has already switched him on.

"Hello Gina," Richard says through the speaker in Red's fingers. I shake my head and say nothing. I'm not doing this, especially in front of a potential customer. "Gina? I know you're there. Anyway, I've forwarded the docs to Full Lives, and I could maybe swing by sometime this afternoon and – "

"No. You won't," I say, and even if she claims to be dead, Red is savvy enough to know to switch the speakerphone off.

The rest of their conversation goes on somewhere in Red Posy's own circuitry, and when the call is over, her eyes meet mine.

"We can get going?" she says, with a subtle upward turn in her soft voice, just unsure enough for it to still be a question.

HeartCorps, on the west side of town, was one of the first to fund a developmental arms race for NextState people. It didn't really matter who started it, because the artificial intelligence they produced gained momentum at such dizzying rates that there was no way to unplug and stop the experiment. The NS had structured their own corporation before the first physical android carrier was built. Suddenly there they were, fully formed, human shaped, and living a parallel existence to us. Even the energy powering Full Lives comes from an NS-operated solar farm. Perhaps because it happened so fast, there was really nothing to be done about it. No violence, no computers demanding that we OBEY – just a thing that happened.

At any rate, all that doesn't really explain why the person lying on my gurney put herself there. Kathleen tries to keep up the small-talk and it's going nowhere.

"So have you lived here in Blakely long?" she asks, looking into the rearview.

"Um…"

"Or rather, *did* you live in Blakely long?"

"I don't really understand," she says.

Rush hour traffic passing HeartCorps has Aster Street backed up a bit with some particularly rude people switching off the auto and trying to make passes, slowing everyone down.

"That dress is a lovely choice," I say, hoping that Red will ignore Kathleen's questions. I shoot Kathleen a glare.

"It is stunning with that shade of red," she says.

"Thank you," Red says. I see her stirring on the gurney in the reflection in the mirror, like she's trying to get comfortable.

We wheel her out of the coach and into the elevator to our basement with the cool storage holding and embalming rooms. We do this on autopilot until I realize that Red doesn't need to be kept cold, and embalming would probably really mess with her circuitry. I push Red into the holding room, right next to the other three sheet-covered corpses.

"Okay then," I say. "Here we are." Red sits up and looks around. She stares at the bulge in the white sheet next to her.

"Don't forget the Guillorys are coming shortly," Kathleen says. "While we wait, I'll get to Mrs. Grayson's makeup." Before I can respond, she makes her escape to the opposite end of the room for makeup prep.

"Can we maybe talk about our plans?" Red asks me. "Should I have a bed sheet?" The poor girl looks so lost that for a moment I forget that she's threatening a lawsuit if this doesn't go well. I ask Red to follow me up to my office. Instead of her footfalls clanking, she steps completely silently, so that I find myself checking back again and again as we walk down the hall to my office, each time her eyes fix firmly onto mine and I have to push on a smile.

In my office, Red sits at the chair across from me. I take a sip of my lukewarm coffee and watch as Red thumbs through a catalog of caskets.

"We have only a small showroom," I say, though it doesn't seem like we're here to talk caskets. I run through my routine anyway because the quiet is making me uneasy. "But we can custom order just about anything to suit a wide range of budgets, especially if time is not an issue."

Red closes the catalog. With her slender red fingers, she fidgets with the wide strap on her shoulder, still staring down.

"I expect that you're curious about how I died," she finally says. "Cause of death can determine an open or a closed casket in some cases, yes." What the hell am I saying?

I look at my monitor and see that I've been typing nonsense into the various fields in some subconscious attempt to look productive. I force myself to lift my hand from the keys and take a moment to look at Red. Her face is smooth and flexes distinctly with every minute expression. The way she looks tense around her sharp jaw line below her ears, contracting and relaxing, so lifelike, it's as if the red paneling is only makeup atop a human.

The parts between the panels, the ones that look so lively, I assume must be filled with fluids, pressurizing and draining in microsecond-responses to signals and computations. In this, she's already so much like the bodies downstairs, pumped full of fresh embalming fluid for that illusion of life.

Mercifully, she ignores my response. She leans back in the chair.

"Do you like movies? I very much used to like movies. I have seen quite a lot. Have you ever seen *Finding Nemo?*"

"Um, what?"

"There's this fish and his mother is killed. Then the fish gets lost and the father goes on an adventure to recover his son."

"Uh huh," I say. My mother had taken me to see it when I was a kid, but something about hearing a machine retell it startles me. I feign confusion so she'll go on.

"It's beautiful, the colors. There is a lot of love, and humor, and the time is managed marvelously. Each of the fish learns something important about their lives on their journey. In the end, the son is found."

"Good," I say.

"Yes," she says. "I was glad too."

There is a pause, then, that goes on for what seems like ages. I hear the casket lift operating and know that Kathleen is getting ready for the Guillory visitation.

"You don't understand," Red says, the disappointment evident in the rasp in her voice. "There are many stories like this in your culture. When the lost thing is found, everything is restored.

28

The story ends – it has to. Otherwise it isn't a story." She leans forward, and her eyes open very wide. With a crimson finger, she points at her perfect blue iris. A chill rushes over me and I blink hard. It is round and soft and artificial, and yet I can tell that I am looking at *someone*. "I've finished. The things I was to do are done. The other NS back up their experiences, scrap themselves for a remodel, and reupload. But I don't work like that. The time is over and I want to have my ending."

Then she stands, and turns partway so that I see her from behind. She gently lifts up the wiry coils away from her skull. I can see the faint outline of a little rectangle recessed into the head plate. She taps it with a finger.

"A little help, please. Do you have a coin?"

I fish around my top drawer and pull a dollar out. There's a small slot there, and as I hold the coin up, I feel my face flush hot. Though I don't know what is beneath the rectangular door, this feels incredibly intimate. But I want to go further. Hand trembling, I open the metal cover. Beneath it there is a tiny blue button, and a series of pin-sized holes in an array like an audio speaker. I don't know what it is, but it feels wrong to be seeing it.

"It's okay, you can relax," she says warmly. "It only shuts down if you give it the right command. Only the Programmers and I know it. I can't do it myself. It's not favorable behavior to have the choice to exist or not."

"And you don't want to, um, upload into someone else?"

"No. I want a funeral."

Noon approaches, and Mrs. Guillory and two of her sons have arrived, so I send Red back to the basement. She wants to see the wake, so I tell her she can view the security feed if she likes. I sit her down on a spare stool in the storage room near a little monitor I keep overhead for particularly busy times when a visitation is going on.

Kathleen and I greet the bereaved, and the two puffy-eyed Guillory sons both wear suits slightly too small for their big rectangular frames. They sip Mountain Dews in the lounge while Mrs. Guillory talks to the empty body of her husband on the kneeler. As the guests trickle in, I stay in the visitation room and Kathleen greets people out front to show them in.

I can't help but imagine what this must look like for Red. I avoid eye-contact with the cameras in the corners. Paul Guillory, the deceased, was only in his late fifties. He was so frail and gaunt that efforts for a lifelike appearance came up a little short. Still, he isn't terrible looking, bald and thin, but still clearly young, with a smooth face just like in the pictures in the collage we set up in the foyer. I watch as the deceased's best friend clogs up the line behind her, tucking something into Paul's dead hand. I'm always intrigued by those who feel the need to touch the bodies – so long as they don't touch the face and threaten to spoil the illusion for everyone else.

Paul Guillory lies in a pricey mahogany Provincial. I wonder what Red would think of the way he looks in death, or if she likes the idea of a casket. Would she want something less flashy, less organic – metallic like her skin? A young girl bumps into me and jostles me back into focus. I readjust the flowers that are fine the way they are.

As the day drags on, I listen to the stories people tell. They're the usual – about how strong a fighter Paul was and how kind a father he was, about how his life was too short but how he really *lived*, ya know? – but there's something different about how I hear them.

I realize that an odd thought has crept into my mind. I can't shut Red down. I won't.

This is probably going to cause some trouble. I know Richard will use any excuse to call and complain, but I can't be forced to shut anyone down. Assisted suicide? Not the business that I'm in.

By four, the Guillory men and some stray cousins put on gloves to be pall bearers and with their help I've loaded the coach to head towards the Lily Lake cemetery. I go to let Kathleen know we're heading out.

Downstairs, Kathleen is standing over Red Posy under the overhead lamp, applying makeup. Red is half-covered in a white sheet and those perfect, living eyes are closed shut.

"Really, Red," I say, trying to politely tease. "Makeup?"

"It's part of her requests," Kathleen says. She reaches behind her and holds up a sheet of paper. "Everything's outlined and set to go."

"You did that all today?" I ask Red. She still hasn't bothered to open her eyes.

"Last night," Kathleen answers for Red.

This is growing frustrating so I turn to leave. But then I freeze where I am. I look at Kathleen, in her surgical mask and goggles, her hair still neat this late in the day.

"You killed her," I say. Kathleen squints, sets down the foundation brush.

"She told me you wouldn't be able to do it," Kathleen says to me. She sounds annoyed with me, as if we'd had this conversation hundreds of times. "I told her you definitely would."

"And now you owe me ten dollars," Red says, and I feel the air rush out of me. Her eyes open and she moves her head just a bit to look at me. "But really, Gina, you're going to have to eventually." The makeup looks silly on her, shining against the matte red finish. When she sits up, the beaded lipstick runs down her chin. The relief I feel at seeing her move surprises me. Why does it matter to me if she operates or not?

"What does a dead NS do with money, exactly?" Kathleen says.

The interment goes fine – it's a sunny day, and each of the Guillorys comment on how odd that is, for someone to be buried on such a nice day, even though everyone makes a comment about what kind of day it is to be buried, rain or shine. When I return home, Kathleen is in the garage. She has her gym duffel slung over her shoulder, and she gives me a little salute as she gets in her car to leave for the day. Inside the cleaners have already removed the flowers and vacuumed everything well, and I get a text of the invoice. I head to my personal space above Full Lives to prep some dinner.

I have a file in our document folder that Kathleen forwarded me just before leaving. It's the contract for Red Posy's arrangements. She wants a pine casket, and no interment but to be sent back to the NS home where she came from after the funeral. Mrs. Grayson's just about ready but the visitation won't be for another day because her children are out of town. So that makes tomorrow free.

I shudder then at the thought that she is down below me, lying there on a gurney, thinking or doing who knows what. When people meet me, especially on (bad) dates, I'm often asked how I can go to sleep knowing that there are dead bodies in the basement of my home. And then there are the puckered faces when people start to visualize the details of my work. I remind them that they are not the undead, lying in wait to rise up and devour me in my sleep. Inevitably, one of us soon asks for the check. Richard never asked questions like this, but he found other ways to disappoint me.

Which is why having Red in my basement is so unnerving. She claims she is dead, but that sort of throws out my whole perception of what that means. What could she possibly be doing down there amongst the corpses, lying in the gurney next to the fully prepped Penelope Grayson? Dead people aren't supposed to do anything. I don't even know if NS sleep. Maybe there is some kind of internal computer network she logs into, sending last minute invitations to her own funeral.

I am supposed to be the expert on death.

After dinner I grab a collection of comics, something banal and pre-NS, a campy noir on-going series about a group of high school girls who are trying figure out who killed their chemistry teacher. It's great until they stumble upon a second crime scene, and the splashy red looks far too familiar and I feel dizzy and have to put it down. Fitful sleep eventually washes over me and I awaken groggy for the day.

Kathleen comes to my office door the moment I sit down. She has her mask flipped down beneath her chin and her hands on her hips like she's waiting for me to say something.

"So you're ready for this?" she says. I know from her tone that she wants to know if I'm ready to be responsible for shutting Red Posy down.

"Ugh, no." I don't want Kathleen to see me get emotional about a customer but I also don't want to be in any way responsible. "I just want to provide the same services we normally do."

"You're right," she says. "The funeral home shouldn't have to pull the plug. And you're the boss, of course."

She gives a little bow with her hands pressed together and then goes into the basement to ready the casket. I check the visitation room to make sure it's ready. I sign for a delivery of croton plants in wicker baskets that Red had picked out of a catalog. She wanted something that could be put back in the ground – nothing that had to be killed. But then there's a lovely blue hydrangea that we hadn't ordered. The "from" tag is written in the angular script of the NS code. It's easily read by them but we need a special app on our phones. I download it and scan it, but then the result was a mess of text and characters I can't comprehend either.

Downstairs, Red waits in her casket. She looks great, opting to do away with the powders and liquids. There is a sheen to her like a newly waxed car, but it still doesn't make her look like some mechanical thing, which would make everything much easier. Kathleen has twisted the ends of the wires coming from her neatly together with a plastic tie. The bundle lies gracefully over one shoulder.

"Thank you both so much for all the work," Red says, as Kathleen helps adjust the dress while she lies flat. I nod.

The front bell rings. I would have stayed upstairs if I thought someone would come. I leave Kathleen to tend to the lift, and rush upstairs.

And there's Richard, smiling in a way that people usually do not smile at a funeral, even when you haven't seen them for a long time. He's grown out a bushy blond beard in the month since I last saw him in person, and his hair is gelled back. He wears the dark blue herringbone jacket I bought him for his birthday, and though he's probably oozing sweat, he actually looks pretty good with that gray shirt under it.

"Gina!" I brace for an uninvited hug, but he walks past me. He signs the book Kathleen has prepared for Red, to be sent to

Richard after the funeral. When he goes into the visitation room and is out of sight, I take the pen and sign it as well.

I walk into the visitation room, and Richard texts on his phone. There is pulsing music, varying slightly – Kathleen tells me Red picked it out.

"Gina," she says. "You've gotta get downstairs."

I try to calm myself down, knowing what's coming.

"It would be a little embarrassing," I say. "To host a funeral without anyone having died."

I feel the water welling in my eyes and I force a smile – who knows why. Richard looks up from his phone and sees the state I'm in and I see him halfway get up, his leg tucked under awkwardly. That he ultimately stays where he is, that partway gesture, does a lot.

"I didn't think you would come," Red says when I arrive downstairs. She turns to expose the hatch in the back of her head. My fingers touch the dollar coin in my pocket but I leave it there.

"It really needs to be me?" I ask.

"No," she says. "But you were kind. I thought I'd give you the honor."

"Of killing you?"

"The opposite," she says. She turns her head toward me, and those eyes pull me like moons. I notice the coin is out of my pocket and I'm reaching toward the hatch to open it. "I knew you wouldn't make me be a machine forever."

How did I not understand that before? Any other machine could be turned on again, or uploaded into something else. But to be able actually to die means that she was once alive. That's what Red wants. I can do that.

I open the hatch.

"It's Nemo," she says, and laughs a short, joyful laugh. "Push the blue button and say it."

So I do.

I sit on the step near the casket and Kathleen hands me a glass of water. There is nothing but a body in the casket behind me, as always. That's how this is supposed to go – me unshakable, handling all of this.

I'm still bleary-eyed when the first guests come in. They're young and they look excited but serious. I am trying to compose myself and Kathleen springs into action, greeting them, showing them the guestbook. They speak in hushed voices, as people do, but there is something different here. It's awe. Then more people come, and Richard is going on about how the invites he posted online weren't reaching as many viewers as he's paid for, but I'm not really listening. The crowd grows bigger, and there are even a few NS entering, drawing stares from the guests. The music plays on, and without even really noticing the shift, I'm greeting the guests, shaking hands. A teenage girl with baggy jeans and a black t-shirt takes my hand.

"I'm sorry for your loss," she says.

"Thank you," I say.

People pour in and out all day long. There are reporters waiting politely in the parking lot asking for comments from guests. This is exactly what Red wanted to happen.

When the crowds finally thin, I approach the casket. Red lies beautiful as ever, shiny silicone eyelids closed. I think of what Red said, how this is what separates her from a machine.

I touch her smooth, cold hand.

Tonight we will return Red Posy to the NS neighborhood to be scrapped for recycling. I'll drive home and I'll probably sleep terribly. Tomorrow Mrs. Grayson's family will arrive, and we will lift her up from the basement. She was old and loved, so there will be a good-sized crowd but nothing out of the ordinary. Mr. Grayson plans to play guitar, some of her favorites, for the family to listen to. He is worried if that would be okay. I tell him it's fine.

Tony Clavelli is an ESL teacher, stop-motion animator, and freelance writer from Illinois. His stories have appeared in *Metaphorosis, The Oddville Press, Jersey Devil Press,* and *The Awl.*

Apocalypse Beta Test Survey

Gregg Chamberlain

Greetings, **gentlebeing**, or whatever current alternative non-gender-specific address form is acceptable, and please excuse this interruption of your dream-state as we at Armageddon Inc. – where our motto is "The Horsemen are *always* ready to ride!" – ask you to consider taking part in a new project, inasmuch as our psychological profile indicates you may be someone with the potential interest and inclination to be part of a select subjects group to assist us in the beta-test of our new designer doomsday line of product services, which we are planning to introduce given the overwhelming popular appeal of the recent Mayan Calendar crisis, though this time we can assure one and all that every possible glitch is worked out to avoid a repeat of that fiasco, and also we can now offer a wide choice of cataclysms that will fulfill any apocalyptic fantasy, featuring such perennial favourites as: World War Three, with or without the atomic orbital bombardment option, along with ecological catastrophe, nuclear winter, solar flares or a full speeded-up expansion of the sun, plus we have a plethora of pandemic possibilities, and a new selection of current cutting-edge fads like robotic revolution, the biblical Judgment Day or other theological visions of doom like the Norse Ragnarok, complete with the Fimbul Winter, or, for the more intellectually-inclined, total global economic chaos, and, of course, we do have traditional fan favourites like alien invasion along with both a standard and a deluxe version zombie apocalypse, and all of these have a 100-per cent satisfaction guarantee with this no-risk trial offer or Armageddon Inc. promises to restore your space-time continuum to its current steady-state setup, minus an acceptable minimum of collateral damage or change based on our certified accounting department's calculations, and so before we return you to your theta-rhythm REM session, please take a nano moment to consider and take quick advantage of this exclusive, one-time-only, unique opportunity, our operators are standing by ready for your virtual signature on the contract, so be the first in your demographic to end the world before someone else beats you to it, and please note this offer may be void, prohibited or subject to certain restrictions on some planes of the multiverse, and with that cautionary note we thank you for your time and attention and if you will just submit yourself now to our customer survey satisfaction scan, totally painless we assure you, then we will once again thank you for your cooperation, wishing you good luck, and a nice life, however it might end.

Gregg Chamberlain sometimes has strange dreams, which explains this story, at least so he says. He lives with his missus, Anne, in rural Eastern Canada, which they share with a clowder of cats. What the cats think and dream about when they sleep they do not share with the humans.

Spirejack

Patrick Warner

Art: Siobhan McDonald
Sponsored by Martyn Turner

Soaring as they did into the unending cloud, the spires might be beautiful if viewed in the right way. That being the case, Kim Brenner must have been looking at them wrong. No doubt it was another story up top, in the great gardens of the hub cities above the ash cloud, but from down here they were just dirty great pylons propping up a volcanic sky.

He yawned, peering through the grubby windshield as the damaged trunk of Spire 12,164 hove into view. He wondered why a simple coolant leak had required him to punch in at four in the morning. Still, Section had promised him double time, so here he was, out in the wastes. He rubbed mulch from the corners of his eyes, stuck in the autumn of waking. His seasons were a mess. He knew he was going to spend the day trudging through winter drifts and that the spring would come just before sleep, making for beautiful summer dreams. But they would only be dreams, and when he woke it would be autumn once more, the cold nipping at his heart, which would be frosty and leafless by lunchtime. God, he missed her.

Seasons were at the front of Kim's mind this morning. He'd fallen asleep watching Midori's archived recordings of old nature documentaries, lulled by sweeping vistas and the narrator's comforting, baritone certainty. It'd be something to see blue sky, Kim thought. White snow, rather than grey; the shock of colour in spring and autumn; greenery.

Grumbling at every juddering impact of the bird-like mechanical legs beneath the cockpit, Kim shifted his walker up a gear. It lurched into an uncomfortable gallop that trammelled the grey, featureless dirt between him and the horizon. Midori had always seen potential in the wastes, but they were pure barrenness to Kim. That was how she always slipped into his thoughts – her opinions persisted where she did not.

Kim's radio crackled into life. He grabbed the transceiver, grateful for distraction.

"You nearly there, Kim? Over," rasped a voice stifling a thin, metallic yawn.

"Few miles out yet. Over."

"Ok. Ping when you're on site. Over."

"Will do. Over."

"Sorry it's such an early one. Over."

"No problem, Section. Somebody's got to do it. Out."

The walker lumbered onward through the illumination grid. Huge stacks of lights winked out as Kim passed, others flaring into life ahead to brighten his path. He crested the steep hillock from which Spire 12,164 extruded like a colossal hair from a giant follicle, pinged his location back to Section and powered down the walker. Its avian knees bent back and upward, lowering the cockpit to ground level. He was half way out the door when the speakers crackled again.

"Kim? You still there? Over."

"Still here. Something wrong, Section? Over."

"Nothing wrong. Apparently someone from topside is meeting you. Over."

"Topside?" Kim didn't listen to Section's reply, instead apprising a short man who rounded the trunk of the spire and waved at the walker. He wore an expensive looking green coat over white overalls, and his symmetrical features seemed squeezed into too small a space at the centre of his face. "Yeah, I see him. What's he doing here? Over."

"No idea. Got told to expect him, is all. Be nice, ok? Over."

"Sure," said Kim, frowning as he waved back at the topsider. "Is he with a Ministry? Over."

"You know as much as I do. Ping again when the job's done. Out."

Kim replaced the transceiver, grabbed his tools and hopped out the door, dropping the few feet to the grey earth below.

"Kim, is it?" said the short man, brightly.

"Yes, sir," said Kim, taking in the green and white accoutrements that indicated the man was from the Ministry of Judgement.

"Oh, please. No need for honorifics," the little man scoffed, fussing with his lapels.

"Alright," said Kim, biting off the contemptuous 'sir' that tried to spill from his lips. "What can I do for you?"

"Oh, I'm just here to supervise."

"Excuse me?"

"Not that you aren't completely competent, I'm sure." Kim's brow furrowed and the little man added "No offense meant, obviously."

"I can do my job."

"Then perhaps I misspoke. I'm here to observe." There was a slickness to the way the little man corrected himself that belied his fussy manner. Kim felt unaccountably wrong-footed by him.

"Whatever you say, boss."

"Please, please—"

"No honorifics, sure," said Kim. "Have you..." he gestured to the spire.

"Yes! Yes, the coolant leak is around the far side. Let me show you."

Kim followed the topsider around the trunk of the spire in silence, nodding and smiling whenever the little man commented on some fascinating feature of the architecture or machinery. "You've not seen the trunks before?" Kim asked, eventually.

"What? Oh, yes, many times. Not in person, of course," said the little man, waving a hand dismissively.

"What do you mean?"

"I've seen pictures, structural blueprints, all the architectural holos. I'm considered something of an authority in hub circles." The corners of the little man's mouth tightened in a smile that didn't touch the rest of his face.

"Are you?" said Kim, offering a more complete version of the same expression.

"Certainly," said the little man, puffing out his concave chest, which conspired to make him look pot-bellied. "Obviously the kind of hands-on experience you've got would be a great boon but…"

"Not a job for topsiders, sure."

The little man sputtered something that might have been apology, justification or outrage. Kim didn't particularly care. It didn't pay to get tangled up with topsiders.

"I didn't catch your name," Kim said.

"Milo," said the topsider.

"Pleasure," said Kim, perfunctorily. He pointed to a ragged tear in the trunk. Its curling, razor edges were blackened with soot. "This it?"

"Indeed. Notice anything strange about the damage?" Milo's eyes sharpened as he asked the question.

"No," lied Kim. It seemed wisest to pacify the little man, get the job done and get away from the complications Ministry types introduced. The little man blinked and nodded, his cold smile reappearing. *I will have the truth,* it seemed to say.

A few laborious hours later Kim welded a heavy plate over the incongruously fresh components gleaming within the grubby rent. Milo thanked him effusively for his work, the cracks in his friendly veneer wide and dark. He shook Kim by the hand and watched, waving, as his walker lumbered off into the light-grid.

Once the darkness between motion-sensitive floods separated him from Milo, Kim radioed Section with some more questions about the unsettling little man, none of which were answered. He mentioned that the damage to the trunk didn't look accidental, but that he hadn't wanted to say anything in front of Milo. Section told him to go home while they processed his pay.

It was early evening when he got back to his undercity quarters, walking the last kilometre from the hyperloop, but he crawled straight into bed. His fingers explored the indentation beside him in the mattress, a nightly reminder of the way that Midori used to fidget and snore and take up too much space, and that now she took up none at all. He dreamed summer dreams of their time together and gave no further thought to Milo's strange visit.

The next week was uneventful, except that Kim's calendar reminded him of his fifth wedding anniversary. Stonily, he cancelled the repeat alert. The pain of Midori's continued absence was all he had left of her, but it made him useless. Breaking from it meant either conceding that he was a widower, or a concerted regimen of distraction. Only one option was viable.

He fell into his work – provided he was exhausted, sleep came dreamlessly. He worked more and slept less. A month passed before he heard mention of Milo again.

As she spilled out of a dive bar on the edge of the meat culturing district, Dana Fenchurch asked whether Kim had heard that a little man in a green coat was asking questions about him and snooping around the HR department.

Bernard Derry asked him the same question a week later as they rode the hyperloop together. Kim said no, again, and disembarked at the next station, fretting about the Ministry of Judgement.

Pushing along the crowded platform, Kim slipped between two burly men who were ripe with the stink of fungus farming, and pressed through the turnstiles. Tacking away from the crowd of commuters and skirting the city proper, he cut through the open market to the east. The roof of the undercity was high enough for its smooth grey surface almost to resemble the cloud cover Kim so admired in his nature documentaries. The air was thick with the smells of spice and old meat, which lingered low, competing for attention as fiercely as the cries of hawkers against the roaring rattle of the hyperloop passing overhead.

Kim stomped through the red light district which fringed the market and out into the dense residential grid, his thoughts swirling. He arrived at his quarters in the spirejack district to find his door ajar, spilling light into the hall. Movement cast a shadow over his hand, outstretched to the lock. He pulled back, breath shallow, wondering what intruder would be so careless as to let their presence be so visible. Could it be Milo? His blood rose at the thought of the little man sifting through Midori's things, at the indignity which continued to compound his sorrow. He waited for another movement within, then threw the door open. He burst into his modest dwelling ready for almost anything, except the smiling young girl he found sitting at the table, swinging her legs happily while peering at the remains of Kim's dinner from the previous night.

"This smells bad," she said. Her expression made it clear she thought her presence far less noteworthy than the drying leftovers. "Are you going to eat it?" Kim stared at her, blankly, taking in the pristine white and green of her dress, the expensive shoes, the complex arrangement of her dark curls, the smooth, unmarked skin. "Daddy says you do different things down here, maybe like eating nasty food. Do you eat nasty food?"

"No," said Kim, surprising himself with his urge to respond to the girl's polite but certain tone. She was clearly used to being answered. She cocked her head and looked at the plate again.

"Then why do you have it?"

"I didn't clean my plate after dinner," said Kim, stepping inside and pushing the door to.

"Why?"

"Who are you?"

"Why didn't you clean your plate?"

"I was tired," Kim snapped, finding himself as much compelled by her manner as by a desire to prevent her repeating the question. "What are you doing in my apartment?" He gave the room a cursory scan. Nothing seemed to be missing.

"Why were you tired?"

"I was up early, working." He examined the lock for signs of damage. "How did you get in here?"

"That was this morning, not yesterday. Why were you tired yesterday?"

"How do you know I was up early this morning?" The girl ignored him, scratching at some of the dried sauce on the plate.

"Daddy says you're like moles. Mole people, he calls you. I thought this might be mole food."

"It isn't."

"I've never seen a mole. Have you?"

The absurdity of Kim's defending last night's dinner to a strange little girl foisted itself upon him. "I made this," he said, seizing the plate. "It's food. Old food. My food. In my apartment. Who are you?"

"I'm Mila," said the girl, smiling.

"Well, Mila, this is my apartment and I'd like to know what you're doing here."

"I came to see you."

"To see me?"

"Yes. I was curious about you. Daddy made you sound strange. He talks about you a lot, you know."

"And who's your daddy? Does he know you're here?" said Kim, wanting nothing more than to be able to identify, contact and locate the girl's parent, returning her to him before anyone missed her.

"My daddy's called Milo. I'm seven years old, silly. I can go where I like. He doesn't mind."

"Milo?" Kim's gut twisted at the name. If he had found Ministry scrutiny difficult to stomach before being discovered with an official's child sequestered in the undercity, what was coming would be unbearable. He should throw her out; have nothing more to do with either of them, he thought, though he knew he wouldn't. The undercity was no place for a child on her own.

"He said I could come and look at you if I wanted. He said I had to learn judgement."

"Judgement," repeated Kim.

"Of course, silly," said Mila, spreading her Ministry dress in a seated curtsy.

"You shouldn't be travelling alone."

"Why?"

"You might get hurt."

"No I won't. I've got Pencil." The little girl indicated a tiny object hovering over her left shoulder which Kim had failed to notice. It was roughly six inches long, narrow and pointed, like its namesake, but Kim recognised it for what it was – a Guardian drone. He knew little about the technology which powered such machines but he knew it was a more effective bodyguard than any which might be hired in the undercity. The little drone bristled with nanoweaponry and was more than capable of deciding to use it. Mila examined Kim's face while he stared at Pencil. "You don't look like a bad man," she said. She held up a picture that had been resting in her lap, a picture of Kim and Midori the night they first met. Midori had tracked it down and given it to him for their first anniversary. Mila screwed up her eyes as though to see the picture differently, then sighed and said "She doesn't look like a bad lady."

"She wasn't," said Kim.

"Daddy says she's a bad lady. He says you know where she is."

Kim's skin prickled at the implicit revelation. Midori was alive. "Doesn't he know where she is?" he asked, controlling his voice.

"No. He wants to know, but he doesn't." Mila set the picture down on the table, propping it up so the faces looked both at her and Kim. "He says she killed someone. He said she makes bombs."

"She didn't. She doesn't."

"Really?"

"She got caught up with some bad people." He didn't know why he was explaining himself like this to a seven year old girl, the hovering threat of the Guardian drone notwithstanding, but for something in her look and her tone which made him feel unburdened.

"What do you mean?" Mila's eyes were wide and clear. Perhaps her judgment was as unpolluted as her gaze. Perhaps she and the drone were here to compel him to lie, but Kim felt suddenly like she deserved the truth.

"She tried always to stand up for people. Then she met a group of people who said they felt the same, but they lied. They wanted to make life better for themselves, even if it made things worse for others. They did some bad things and it looked like Midori had done them too, but she hadn't. I know she hadn't." Kim remembered the last conversation he had with Midori, the strange, benign, distant affection he'd felt from her the night before the Ministry came asking about the others, the night before she was gone. He remembered how important it had seemed to her that he knew her better than anyone. None of it made sense until the accusations had poured through the door in a white and green tide the next day, upturning his life with heavy boots and careless hands. "She only wanted to help people. She would never have hurt anyone."

"She sounds nice."

"She was."

"Daddy didn't make her sound nice."

"He doesn't know her."

Mila and Kim looked at one another for a long time in silence. She had no prejudices, neither about him nor Midori, only what she had been told and, in the manner of children, she had yet to decide whether she believed it. She broke the silence after a few minutes only to say "Tell me about her."

Kim did. It had been so long since Midori had been declared anathema, since he had spoken freely about her, that the opportunity felt like a levee breaking inside him. He talked about the night they met. He talked about how she saw the world and the way her view coloured and shaded the line drawing of his life. He showed Mila her poems. He showed her the sacrosanct imprint of her body on the other side of the bed. He cried without noticing, unable to stop speaking and all the while the strange little girl looked him dead in the eye and seemed to drink in every detail. Later she washed the crusted plate for him while he sat at the table by the stove, talking about her laugh, her love, her face, the feel of her hair. He didn't stop speaking until he had done Midori what little justice words and tears were able. When he finished, Mila stood up, straightened her dress and tugged one of her neat curls out of place so that her high coif toppled into a lopsided beehive.

"I believe you," she said. "Midori sounds nice. I wish you knew where she was. I wish for you, not for Daddy, even though he wants to know. I have to get ready for the responsibility of being born into the Ministry, and understand the privilege of being a topsider, he says. He said I had to make my first judgement on you, so I'm going to tell him to leave you alone, and to stop looking for Midori. I think I'd like her if I met her. I hope I get to, one day."

Kim stared at her as she began walking toward the door. "Wait, what you mean?" he asked.

"I've made my judgement," she shrugged. "I'm going to tell Daddy you're not a bad man, even if you are a mole man. I'm going to tell him Midori isn't a bad lady, too. Then the Ministry won't come looking for either of you anymore. I think he'll be proud of me."

"I think he will," said Kim, dumbfounded.

"Maybe Midori will come back, once she knows I believed you. Come on, Pencil." Mila walked out, shadowed by the Guardian drone. She waved back through the door, then closed it daintily. Kim slumped into his chair and laughed until tears coursed down his face. Could it really be so simple, so absurd? The world was messy, and often ugly, but sometimes it was beautiful too.

She *will* come back, he thought. I know she will.

Patrick Warner is a young actor who has been writing for a little over a year. He has had success with his short fiction since then, with his most recent work forthcoming at www.theshortstory.co.uk.
When touring doesn't relegate him to strangers' spare rooms he lives in London, where he is currently working on a novel.

The Last Moonshot

Vaughan Stanger

Art: Becca McCall

Jessica frowned as she gazed at the Moon's gleaming face. "Daddy, why is *this* moon so bright?"

Not for the first time, she had been caught raising the window's shutter long after she'd been tucked into bed.

"The Moon looks normal to me, Jessie," Daddy said, as he snapped his fingers to first lower and then lock the shutter again. "But in any case, you *really* should be asleep by now."

Jessica sighed. Daddy calling her "Jessie" was nearly as bad as not answering her questions. Hearing footsteps on the landing, she turned around and asked Mummy instead.

"Jessica is right," said Mummy. "There was an article about it on my news-feed this morning. Tonight's full moon *does* look bigger than normal, which also makes it brighter. Astronomers call it a Super Moon."

Jessica frowned at her. "How many moons *are* there? Cos the one I saw on my birthday looked like a slice of melon."

Daddy chuckled. "Jessie darling, there is only one moon."

Jessica was pleased to see Mummy give Daddy one of her looks.

"Let's see if we can figure it out together," said Mummy. "And let's see if Daddy can operate the holo-projector correctly this time."

After watching the animations Mummy found for her, Jessica was willing to accept that the Earth only had one moon. But learning about its phases left her eager to know more. Having promised Daddy that she would *definitely* go to sleep this time, she waited until the house was completely quiet. Only then did she pull her pad out from under her pillow.

There was so much more she wanted to learn about the Moon.

* *

Jessica pouted her annoyance as laughter rippled around the Year Five classroom.

"But the Earth *does* have two moons!"

"There is only one Moon, Jessica," said Ms Williams, who seemed to be struggling to keep a straight face.

Jessica rolled her eyes. "I *can* prove it!"

"Bet you can't!"

Jessica glared at Oliver Castelow, who sat three places to her left.

"You just watch me!"

A finger-tap on her pad brought up an animated hologram of the Earth-Moon system, which rotated slowly above her desk before zooming in on a tiny speck. That was good enough to silence most of the class, but not Oliver.

"Well, if you're going to count something *that* little!"

Ms Williams made ineffectual shushing noises before asking, "Does this, um, *temporary* moon have a name?"

"No, it's too small," Jessica said.

Ravi Shaktar chose this moment to join in the fun. "Let's call it Jessica's Lump!"

Oliver's pint-sized pal leered at Jessica for extra effect. She turned away just in time to see Tamara Montgomery flick a spitball at her moon.

"Now she's got two," Tamara said, with a pitying glance towards Jessica. Her pigtails shook while she giggled.

Jessica took no notice, even though everyone except Ms Williams was laughing.

Ms Williams slapped the palms of her hands against her desk. "Right, I want everyone to quieten down now!" When the noise had decreased sufficiently, she looked towards Tamara. "Let's see what you've learned about the Earth's *real* moon, shall we?"

Jessica rolled her eyes. Ms Williams wouldn't get anything out of Tamara, who showed more interest in the schoolyard's weeds than the sky above her head.

When Tamara delivered the blank look Jessica had expected, Ms Williams scanned the rest of the class.

"Anyone?"

Ever polite, Jessica raised her hand. Ms Williams nodded towards her.

"I can tell you the year of the *last* moon-landing."

Oliver snorted. "Teacher's pet!"

Jessica knew better than to rise to the bait.

"Needs putting down," said Ravi.

But sometimes the opportunity was too good to resist.

"What – like your sister's cat?"

Ravi responded with his usual scowl while whispering a threat to do the same to her. Jessica shrugged and turned back to Ms Williams.

"It was 1972."

✳ ✳

Despite agreeing with the sentiment, Jess had chosen not to join in with the collective groan provoked by Mr Mbeki's suggestion. She had a much better idea, but needed to pick the right moment.

"What's the point of launching *another* Lego man on *another* weather balloon?" Ollie Castelow asked. "Your class did that last year!"

Jess gave Ollie a quizzical look. This was the first time he'd shown any real interest in a science project. Not that this change-of-heart made putting her in the same Year Nine class as him feel right.

"Why can't we do something *rad* for once?" Ravi Shaktar waved his phone. "Like uploading Ollie's brain onto this!"

Mr Mbeki shook his head. "Because there are ethical considerations, that's why. Does anyone have another suggestion?"

Aware that she might not get another chance, Jess raised a hand. Mr Mbeki crossed his impressively tattooed forearms. His frown suggested he knew what was coming.

"What do you propose, Ms Lambert?"

"For a start, I think we should aim a *lot* higher than thirty kilometres."

Her response drew a nod from Mr Mbeki and more groans from her classmates.

"Okay, then," he said. "Please show us what you have in mind."

"The European Space Agency is looking for student projects that could piggyback on one of its spacecraft," Jess said. "This is what I've come up with."

She ignored the predictable barrage of complaints and activated the simulation. A hologram presenting the launch of an Ariane 7 multi-stage rocket filled the classroom. She followed it with an animation of the deployment of a phone-sized spacecraft that would fly all the way to the Earth's newest temporary moon.

"Wow!" said Ollie. "Now that *is* rad!"

Jess allowed herself to smile, but Mr Mbeki dashed her hopes with a shake of his head.

"So, if we exclude those ideas that are illegal or too ambitious that leaves us with either the high altitude balloon or Ms Montgomery's proposal for glow-in-the-dark sniffer rats. Okay, let's put them to the vote…"

The wail of the bio-attack siren halted the show of hands for the balloon option, which Jess had reluctantly decided to support. Annoyingly, the alert, which turned out to be only a drill, swayed the majority of the class into supporting Tam's proposal, which did not interest her at all.

She would have to find another way.

✳ ✳

55

Dressed in wearables she'd scavenged from the 'hood's overflowing skips and sporting an e-visor to match, Jess trusted that she looked sufficiently gang-related to satisfy her former classmate.

"What I want to do, Ollie, is build a rockoon."

"It's 'OC' now! And don' you forget it!"

She guessed that his hand gestures indicated his annoyance at being addressed by his pre-initiation name. Not that Jess cared. She'd call him anything he wanted if it helped achieve her goal.

"Okay, 'OC'. You got something I can use?"

"What you want a raccoon for anyway?" OC narrowed his gaze. "You doin' GM stuff for MoTam now'days?"

Exasperation made Jess look up at the sky. Working for MoTam? No way!

"A *rock*oon, shit-for-brains, is a balloon-launched *rocket*."

OC screwed up his face while making handgun gestures. "I knew tha'!"

Yeah, right, she thought, but refrained from saying. Still, at least she had caught his attention. OC had always liked anything that made a loud noise, hence his choice of gang.

"So tell me, what kind of ordinance are your Bang-Tech buddies packing these days?"

"Tha's strictly 'need to know'!"

She punched his left shoulder, hard. OC winced but stood his ground.

"Well, *I* need to know!"

OC puffed out his chest in an attempt to look the part. He wasn't fooling anyone, least of all her.

"You'll have to swear allegiance."

She managed a grin despite the rumours she'd heard about the Bang-Techs' initiation ceremonies.

"You lead the way."

✳ ✳

After two years of turf-wars and technological piracy, JL relished the prospect of stepping down as leader of the Bang-

Techs. Working on a gang-exit placement at Virgin Galactic would seem like the quiet life in comparison. She wouldn't be sorry to lose the e-tats.

"We're good-to-go," OC said.

She would miss him of course. Then again, if everything went to plan, she wouldn't miss him at all.

JL tapped an icon on her mil-spec phone. Released from its tether, the weather balloon dragged its payload a few metres along the churned-up ground before hoisting it into sky the colour of lead.

Not long now.

Not long, too, for her nemesis-in-waiting to deliver his promised revenge. She'd booted Ravi out of the Bang-Techs one week after taking over his GetLoaded collective. Since then, disturbing rumours had reached her about an alliance with MT and her Gene-Genie crew.

She gazed at the vid-feed displayed in her visor, while the overlaid graphics kept her informed about key mission events. She punched the air when the rocket fired just seconds after the balloon burst, sending BTG-1 on its way. Moments later, the 'hood's siren shrieked a warning.

QC yelled, "Incoming!"

A deafening explosion terminated his dash for cover.

Peppered with shrapnel and already struggling to breathe, JL made a half-hearted grab for her gas mask, then let it slip from her fingers. Her only regret was that she wouldn't survive long enough to watch the solar sail unfurl.

She continued to watch the video feed until her brain frothed into soup.

* *

JL* congratulated herself on a problem-free reboot while bump-bumping the miniature mannequin her mind now occupied around what remained of Lambert2033.

Six months had passed while the BTG-1 photon-tacked its way towards the lorry-sized moonlet left over from the Solar System's formation. After harpooning its target, the spacecraft activated

57

its rock processor and began extracting metals and organics. Some hours later, the 3D printer began disgorging parts for the assembler to piece together.

JL* was pleased with the result.

Only one thing was missing.

After checking that sufficient feedstock remained, JL* commanded the printer to build her a companion.

* *

With only two hours left before Lambert2033 slipped from Earth's gravitational grip, JL* knew what she wanted to do. Unfortunately OC* had other ideas.

<< Reckon it's 'bout time we headed home! >>

JL* shook her head.

<< Do you *really* want to melt on re-entry? >>

OC* gestured towards the Moon.

<< Okay... So how 'bout we go out with a bang? >>

Granted, if BTG-1 detached from Lamber2033 it could employ its solar sail to accomplish a crash-landing, but that outcome too held no appeal for JL*. After all, Humanity had been to the Moon already.

<< I've got a *much* better idea. >>

<< Gonna let me in on it? >>

JL* nodded.

<< Let's do nothing! Let's continue riding this rock and see where it takes us. >>

After a moment's consideration, OC* responded with a grin.

<< You rule, girl! >>

Indeed she did.

Formerly an astronomer and more recently a research project manager in an aerospace company, **Vaughan Stanger** now writes SF and fantasy fiction full-time. His stories have appeared in *Daily Science Fiction, Abyss & Apex, Postscripts, Nature Futures*, and *Interzone*, amongst others. Follow his writing adventures at www. vaughanstanger.com or @VaughanStanger.

Duncan Lunan

The Elements of Time

Sydney Jordan

Illustrated by Sydney Jordan

Classic time travel stories from the last four
decades gathered together in print for the very
first time in this special edition

Published by Shoreline of Infinity Publications

paperback £10

also in ebook formats

available in all good bookshops or from

www.shorelineofinfinity.com

Lowland Clearances

Pippa Goldschmidt

On the day we were due to move out, I left the flat for the very last time and stood on the pavement. The bags were all packed and the removals company was due to arrive at any moment, but I wanted a last glimpse. Sure, nobody could say it was pretty, but it had been ours. Here, on the edge of Glasgow, the high-rise flats rose out of the early morning mist, their wet concrete shining in the weak sun. Eight tall buildings, all now to be abandoned and the hundreds of people who had (at least until today) lived here, now anticipating a move to the Highlands. They'd told us that in the north there was plentiful housing just standing empty and waiting for us, although it might need a little attention to bring it up to the standards we were used to. But it had original features like stone fireplaces, and it was so cheap! That was the deciding factor. Of course we hadn't actually been able to see this housing yet, it was too remote. They hadn't finalised the public transport. But that was all in hand, they assured us.

And there was no doubt that in some ways I was pleased to leave my old neighbourhood with all the dirt and rubbish just piling up in the streets. Outside our local chippy were heaps of black bin bags lying on top of older bags. Periodically one of them would burst open and release its rotting insides. You never got used to the smell, even the dog threw up whenever I took it for a walk. Only the gulls and rats seemed immune to the reek.

As I continued to wait on that last morning, a van drew closer. I thought at first it was our removals van but as it pulled up I saw it was the type used to transport livestock. It parked right outside our block and the driver leapt out. The sides of the van were wire mesh and I could see inside, where there were sheep all tightly packed together like a woolly jigsaw puzzle. I felt sorry for them, wondering if they were on their way to the abattoir and if the man had just got lost. There was writing on the side of the van just below the wire mesh, it said 'Dolly Enterprises'.

The man looked a bit confused when he saw me standing there, "I was told you lot'd be gone by now."

"We're just waiting," I told him, "we won't be long." I wondered what exactly he had been told.

"No matter. They won't care," and he pointed at the van's occupants. Then he went around the back and eased out a bolt on the mesh gate so that it slowly swung open and a ramp slid down to the road. The sheep nuzzled one another for a bit, as if trying to encourage each other to make the first move. Then finally the boldest started clattering down the ramp, its hooves loud in the morning air. The rest all followed, about twenty of them.

I was astonished. "What are you doing?" I asked the man, "You can't let sheep loose here, there's no grass for them."

But even as I watched, I noticed the first sheep trot over to the bin bags and start to nibble at an opening in the plastic. A gull perched on top tried to stand its ground, but soon gave up and flew off. The sheep stuck its head right into the bag and I watched as it chewed the contents. Mars bar wrappers, pizza boxes, Irn Bru cans, everything disappeared into the sheep's open mouth and was ground up by its capable teeth. Indeed, its teeth were extraordinarily large, larger than I'd ever seen in any other sheep. Perhaps it was a special breed. Again, the other sheep followed and soon they were all standing around quite contentedly, like farmyard animals tucking into a bale of hay. Then our own removals van showed up and after that I was too busy to carry on watching.

Our journey took longer than expected and when we finally arrived I was disheartened to see just how much work our future home would need. Why, nobody could have lived here for well over a hundred years! The roof had completely caved in and the walls were covered with slimy moss. The house had clearly never had a bathroom, either. But we'd been given a caravan to stay in while we completed the renovations, so we just had to get on with it.

And we'd also been given a few packets of seeds to get the vegetable patch going. At first it was tough, nothing to eat but home-grown kale and spuds with occasional deliveries of oatmeal and herring, but then I remembered some of my granny's recipes from the old days and we got on fine. I told the rest of the family, *you just have to adapt to your surroundings*.

Now, at least we get lamb chops and mutton in the deliveries. And the meat's very cheap, although it does have an odd, almost metallic, aftertaste. Still, we feel quite settled. I can just see us staying here for some time.

Pippa Goldschmidt enjoys writing fiction about science. She's the author of the novel *The Falling Sky* and the short story collection *The Need for Better Regulation of Outer Space*. In 2016, she was a winner of the MRC Suffrage Science award and her poem 'Physics for unwary students' was chosen to be one of the Scottish Poetry Library's Best Scottish Poems.

The Sky is Alive

Michael F Russell

Art: Stuart Beel

Today's problems: The replacement part for one of the harvesters was the wrong size; the service company hadn't repaired the Weather Sat; and the wind was still blowing from the east.

On days like this, Louis Derwent, founder and chief executive of Derwent Organics, was convinced he'd made a terrible mistake. The solution to his predicament was obvious and attractive.

He should sell up and go back to Earth.

That's it: Let his employees take their chances. They should never have answered his advert anyway.

Louis was roused by a wet snout and tongue slathering his cheeks and mouth.

"Get down, for Christ's sake." Disgusted, he pushed the young Alsatian away, jumping to his feet to wipe the drool off with a sleeve. "Kelvin, you know Max isn't allowed in my office – Kelvin!"

There was no answer from his son, so Louis hit the call button on the main console as he shooed the dog out of the door and back down the observation tower's metal staircase. Max scampered a few steps then stopped, eager to return.

"Hi Dad," came the voice over the intercom. "What's up?

"Max – that's what. Come get him. He's in the office. Can't have him jumping up on stuff, or biting wires again."

Kelvin came to reclaim his pet.

"You wanted him, so you look after him," shouted Louis down the stairs. He went back into his office and shut the door more forcefully than he meant to.

He had to watch his temper. It mustn't get the better of him. He was done with angry.

He picked up the scopes and took aim at the east to see what the wind might bring them. He was three floors up and could see clear to the Jackdaw Hills. Closer in, he spotted Amy Chin's tearaway kid on his dirt bike, racing in and out of the gullies near the solar arrays; Alvarez and Pam at the packing depot, flirting with each other. But there was no cloud looming in the distance. The pale pink sky was empty.

He needed better eyes.

He pressed another call button and someone answered.

"Hey boss."

"Frank, the Weather Sat's still down and I've had the same old bull from Colony Solutions. We've had an easterly airstream for days. I'm thinking we should send up a drone. Tell the other farms to do the same, OK?"

"Will do," said Frank.

Ten minutes later Louis had a live feed from 1400 feet as the drone crossed the plain to the Jackdaw Hills. He pushed it higher and turned up the mag.

His heart sank.

"Shit."

With radar mapping from six airborne drones he could see there were three clouds over his land, sweeping due west as they always did. One would cross the outer edge of Trenchborough Farm, 80-miles away, one would pass right across the estate and miss every cropfield and settlement, and one…one was heading straight for Home Farm at a leisurely four miles per hour. It was just under two miles wide and about a third of a mile high; a standard size for a convective flat-top. The first of Gliese 581's mid-year clouds would be here by 4pm.

Louis set the drones on a holding pattern at 4000 feet and opened a hailing channel to every device and public speaker on Home Farm, and in the village.

"Attention people, we have a cloud heading straight for us. Should be here in just over four hours, so get busy in the usual fashion. Don't blame me for the short notice, blame Colony

Solutions. Doug, get out and check the pipe-work between pens seven and eight, last time I looked the ground was damp." He smiled. "And if we can get some focus at the packing depot, ahem, you might want to have a look at the outer hatch on the nearside assembly room, Mr Alvarez. If you can't get it to shut properly use sealant. Look sharp people – incoming."

From his tower-top control room, Louis was satisfied to see the desired response in the compound below. Work-crews formed to secure all the irrigation points, locking hydrants and sprinkler caps and plugging loose hoses. Doug and two others hopped in an argo-jeep, speeding away in a spray of dust and gravel to pen seven. Every dwelling was made secure and every child was called in from wherever they happened to be.

There was a cloud coming.

Louis sat down at his desk. He went through the list of late-payers before rescheduling his own bills, glancing every once in a while at the drone feed to check on the cloud's progress.

After a spell he stood, poured himself a coffee, and went to the window.

Down in the compound, Samantha was trying to arrange her brother and his new dog in an artful pose. Knowing how stubborn she was, Louis was sure she'd ignore the cloud warning until she got her perfect black and white image to add to her study of gritty pioneer folk, at work and at play. But Max kept barking and wouldn't sit still for long enough. The perfect image would have to wait.

A lump came to Louis's throat as he watched his children. He'd wanted to take them on an adventure to the stars. To make them forget what had happened by starting again. But it didn't turn out to be as easy as the agency had said. Because of its axial tilt, Gliese 581 was semi-arid in the tropics, even with the subsurface polar pipes, and no-one had told him about the clouds until the deal was sealed. And service contracts with Colony Solutions weren't worth shit.

He should have bought one of the northern forests with Malia's life insurance and his own severance. It was too cold for the wrong sort of cloud up there. There was also plenty of water, though not that many cash-crops besides timber could grow at mid-latitudes.

It doesn't matter how far you go, pain always comes with you.

He turned towards the stairwell. It was time to get his hands dirty with the others.

In the doorway stood Max, ears erect and tongue lolling, a quizzical look on his face. He wagged his tail.

Louis pointed.

"Out," he said firmly.

The dog's tail wagged to a quicker beat.

"Come on. Move it."

Louis advanced. Max turned and fled, but only down to the next landing, where he waited, his tail still swishing. Once out in the compound Max ran ahead, bounding up to Kelvin, Samantha and her friend, Reena. Before Louis could reprimand his son his daughter spoke.

"I'm gonna stay at Reena's."

Louis tried to look stern. Samantha took his photo.

"I like it. Mean and moody."

"And concerned for his daughter's wellbeing. There's a cloud on its way, you do know that?"

"It's OK, Mr Derwent," said Reena, "Sam's staying at ours."

Louis was almost satisfied. "And your mum knows about this?"

"Yes, Dad," hissed his daughter. "Stop bugging her."

"And Dad," put in Kelvin. "I'm staying at Philip's."

Before Louis could say any more, children and dog ran away. He let them go and checked his wrist-comms, shielding the display from the glare of late-morning Gliese.

"What's the ETA?"

The tower's AI told him two hours and eight minutes, at the current wind-speed, until the cloud reached the packing depot. Louis went back up to his perch and fired off another angry message to Colony Solutions.

A while later he looked up and saw the cloud above the Jackdaw hills, spilling over the summits as it sniffed the parched landscape for the merest hint of water.

Clouds were always thirsty.

Frank powered-down the pumping stations just before the cloud arrived. It moved over Home Farm village, the packing depot fading from view as the curtain of ground-dragging filaments erased the far horizons. Gliese became a faint circle of red star through the cloud's upper vapour haze. Louis felt himself start to sweat. It was always warmer under a cloud.

On the third floor of the tower, he stood at the window, mini-screens showing every webcam in every home and workplace.

"How we all doing?"

A chorus of overlapping reassurances came in from around the village. Everyone was accounted for and every door, window, tap and vent was shut or sealed. No source of water was exposed to the air.

Louis flicked through the various cameras and, as was his habit, turned up the sound on the external ones, pressing his ear to the speaker. The faint hiss he could hear was the hollow hair-thin filaments brushing against the mic. Sometimes, if he listened for long enough, he thought the clouds were talking to him.

He sat up straight again, and selected one of the field cameras. By now the front-edge of the cloud was over the pens and among the trees. Standardised germlines, they were safe under retractable roofs. Personally, he had never taken to the local stuff, though the ones that tasted a bit like bananas were OK.

Cloud filaments were finer than a human hair and hollow, but needle sharp and very strong. A million of them could penetrate any soft surface within seconds. A human body could be drained in a blink, nothing left but a mummified husk. He'd seen it happen. Well, his fruit was safe, and so were the people. But if a cloud found a leak it'd be inside in a flash, and one could rip up a whole pen as the wind pushed it on.

"Hey, Dad, check these out."

Samantha had mailed him some photos. She liked to leave a basin full of water outside when a cloud passed over. She'd been known to get Frank to drive her into the path of one, set up a camera and tripod, and remote-view the results.

Today, the basin was outside her friend's window. The results were stunning, Louis had to admit. As soon as the first filaments had brushed across the water, countless more gathered within seconds to drink. It was as if mist had solidified into the shape of a cone that was emanating from the basin. Each snow-white strand sparkled with pinks and blues as the water rose into the cloud's hot convective core.

"It's lovely, honey, but I wish you wouldn't do that. It's like you're feeding it. Maybe it'll remember if it comes around again."

"That's insane, Dad" said Samantha. "It's just a dumb cloud."

Over the speakers came a shout.

"Max! Ohhh…"

It was Kelvin.

"Son – what is it?" Anxious, Louis checked the screens.

"Dad, it's Max, he got outside. Dad. Fuck. Noooo…"

Louis ran to the window, but he couldn't see more than 20 yards through the drift-net of filaments.

The barking started off as anger but soon became high-pitched yelping, overloading the turned-up speakers. The dog started to squeal, a hideous sound, like the rip of sheet metal. Louis put his hands over his ears. There was movement in the mist, a struggle, a dark shadow jerking in mid-air, in mist that was not mist.

Through the nearest camera, Louis saw.

Already the dog's high-pitched pain had subsided as the cloud lifted him into the air, enfolding him in a billowing white shroud. He let out a soft rattle with his final breath, and a second later his carcass was dropped to the dirt as the cloud relaxed its grip. Max was now a smaller shrivelled thing, a desiccated stick-dog, all ribs and curled up pipe-cleaner limbs. Every molecule of soft-tissue moisture had been extracted from his body.

The cloud drifted on through Home Farm village, on its way to join the northern air-stream migration. There was nothing to do but wait for it to pass.

Louis pressed his face to the damp plexiglass, his palms flat against the window. From the speakers, his son's angry sobs and curses were too loud to bear. The sounds took him back to Earth, back to a different death.

He'd order another dog. Next time he'd be nice to it.

Michael F Russell is a writer and journalist based on the Isle of Skye. His first novel, *Lie of the Land,* was short-listed for the Saltire Society's First Book Award in 2015. His short fiction has appeared in *Shoreline of Infinity, Gutter, Northwords Now* and *Fractured West* magazines.
He is deputy editor of the *West Highland Free Press* newspaper.

The Forever Man, a new Fantasy thriller by author **Allen Stroud**.

"One day I will be too old for the shadows. What kind of monster will I be then?"

One minute Andrew Pryde is in a library, reading; the next, he's staring at the body of a young girl lying between the bookshelves, with a policewoman standing over him. In the blink of an eye, his world has unravelled.

"An engrossing fantasy mystery, bursting with magic and intrigue." Edward Cox

"Stroud has a rare way with words that really engages and disarms the reader." SFBook

Release date 29/09/2017 @ Fantasycon

Academia Lunare is proud to present
Aragorn: JRR Tolkien's Undervalued Hero,
by Angela P Nicholas

"The most enjoyable work on Tolkien I have read in many years" Christina Scull

Aragorn. Strider. King. Ranger. He is one of the most famous and celebrated characters in the history of popular literature. But how much do you really know about the man?

Release date: 15/09/2017

OPEN SUBMISSION WEEK
5th October 17 to 12th October 17

In the month of October, Luna will host its first Open Submission Week, an opportunity to submit your work with a view to receiving a publishing contract. It doesn't matter if you've never been published before, or if you don't have an agent. Your writing skills and creativity are ALL you need.

www.lunapresspublishing.com/submissions

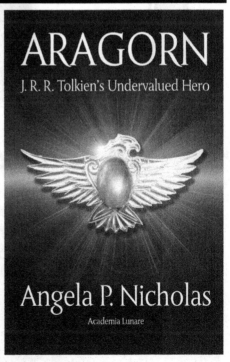

ARAGORN
J. R. R. Tolkien's Undervalued Hero

Angela P. Nicholas
Academia Lunare

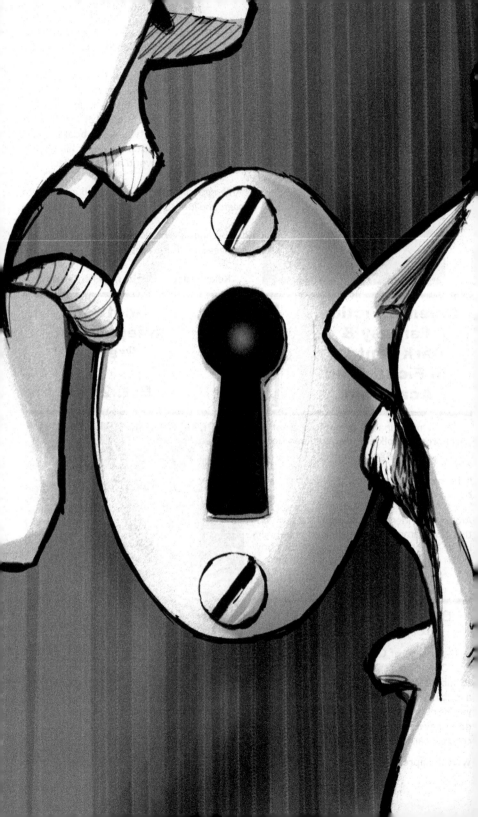

The
Useless Citizen
Act

Ellis SJ Sangster

Art: Monica Burns

Dear Ms R Smith,

The official records of the International Government Administration Office for Scotland tell us that you turn twenty-five years of age before 31ˢᵗ December 2107. As you will be aware, from January 1ˢᵗ to March 31ˢᵗ each year every Citizen between the ages of twenty-five and eighty-five must, by law, comply with all regulations regarding The Useless Citizen Act.

An abridged version of the regulations of the Act is as follows:

1. Every Citizen must be officially employed and able to support themselves as an individual unit without any Governmental or familial support.

2. Every Citizen must be completely free of criminal convictions of grade two or above. Any Citizen with a level one conviction must have completed their Societal Repayment Plan (in accordance with their court order) prior to December 31ˢᵗ of the year in which the conviction was made.

3. Every Citizen must be healthy, and not suffer from any long term physical or mental illness which would cause them to be out of work for more than two months, or that might require excess health care exceeding the £200,000 fund allocated to each Citizen by the International Government at the time of their birth.

Please provide evidence to support your adherence to each of these criteria before 20th December. Citizens located within the Highlands may send Proof of Usefulness to the International Government Administration Office for Scotland, Scottish Highlands Branch, Inverness Castle, View Place, Inverness, IV2 3EG.

If you do not meet these criteria, or cannot obtain a Government approved form of evidence to support your adherence to these criteria, you may expect the arrival of a secondary email within fourteen days which will provide you with your expiration date and time, as well as a pamphlet containing additional, useful information on ways to correctly set your affairs in order.

Yours sincerely,

Lisa Kobb.
Chief Administration Officer for Scotland.

The dark inside the doctor's cupboard is actually quite relaxing. Or it would be if it weren't for the incessant knocking of the nurses on the door. I ignore their polite requests to come out. For the past ten minutes the politeness has been getting sharper, more strained, but I have to admit I'm still impressed it's there at all. I suppose customer service is always important, even when dealing with the condemned.

Another *tap tap* and the voice of an overly friendly woman blows through the keyhole.

"Ms Smith? Ms Smith, you really need to come out now."

No. I don't. Funny thing about death is that it really puts what you *need* into perspective. I apparently *needed* to eat five pieces of fruit and veg a day to help me live longer. Clearly not.

"Ms Smith, please. Open the door."

"There's nothing to worry about, Ms Smith."

"The procedure is completely painless. You won't feel a thing."

"Oh yeah?" I finally find my voice, and I find it defiant. "I'd love to read some of your customer reviews. Better yet, talk to someone who 'knows what I'm going through'."

I do the air quotes despite knowing that none of them can see me. I feel like my body should match my voice, and at least do something a little more interesting than huddle on top of the upturned mop bucket.

There's silence on the other side of the door. Much to my annoyance, I find my ears straining to hear what's going on. Part of me fears what they'll do next now that they've got me talking. The other part of me, the bigger, suddenly braver bit, makes me smile like an idiot simply for knowing I made them speechless.

"Ms Smith," the little, high-pitched chirrup of a voice has an obviously well-practiced, apologetic tone to it. It makes my nose wrinkle, and I cover my head with my hands. My wrists press against my ears, and I listen to rapid beat of the pulse the doctors want to stop. It doesn't block her out. "We are very sorry, but the law states that unless you can prove that you're useful to society then, under The Useless Citizen Act, society is obligated to—"

"Shoot me then!"

"That's not how it's done, Ms Smith." The nurse sounds like an adult talking to a difficult child. The vibrato in her voice gives her a nasty, anxious, tittering tone. "You need to come out of the cupboard now, and—"

"Or what?"

"Or you'll miss your appointment slot." Her tenor darts up an octave. "That's a level four—"

"A level four felony, punishable by, oh yeah! Death! Fuck you!"

"Miss Smith," The short, sharp voice of a man comes through the keyhole. He sounds like one of those types to iron creases into his trouser legs. "Miss Smith, I have to ask you not to swear at my staff. Abuse of our employees is not something we tolerate in this practice, and certainly not by a Useless Citizen."

"What you gonna do? Kill me? Fuck you! Fuck you all! Fuckity-fuck-fuck and fuck you, you fuckers!"

It doesn't help. Even when I imagine the aghast expressions of the nurses, or the dainty, trout-pout receptionist falling side-ways off her swivel chair, it doesn't help. There's a strange feeling in my chest that reminds me of a crack in the earth, only the lava bubbling up from underneath can't decide if it's going to pour out in a flood or burst in a bright, fiery explosion.

"Madam. Your behaviour is inappropriate and—"

"You gonna kick me out, are you?"

"I—" The man's reply is cut short by his own lack of brain power. It's kept short by the hissing whispers of one of the nurses. Probably the shrill one. For a split second, I'm almost hopeful. I swallow the bubbling lava, and just breathe. In through my nose, and out through my dry, volcano mouth. I try and enjoy breathing, or to make the most of it at least. A little voice in my head suggests speeding them up to get more in before I kick the bucket, but I don't particularly want to encourage the panic-attack that's been threatening to choke me for the past few days.

Breathe in. Breathe out. Breathe in. Breathe out. The cleaning cupboard smells of dust and varnished wood.

"Miss?"

I bite my tongue.

"Miss Smith, are you—?"

"Aye. Still alive."

No one laughs.

"I just thought we should tell you that you've missed your appointment. The police have been called to remove you, and will be here soon."

✤ ✤ ✤

Dear Miss R Smith,

Post: Cleaning Operative 3, Inverness Royal Academy (HGH03591)

I refer to your application for the above post.

On this occasion, we must advise you that you have been unsuccessful. We noted with interest your experience and achievements, however, another candidate more closely matched the person specification for this post.

Thank you for your interest in this post and best wishes for the future.

Regards,
Business Support HR C&L

I can feel the crack growing. The bubbling has reached my throat and is forming lumps that I can't swallow. The figments of my imagination pretending to be soot and ash are the things making me sniff and gasp. I'm not crying. I'm not.

"I didn't get it…"

I shrink into the worn cream leather of the armchair. My husband perches on the arm of the chair, reading the email over the top of my head. I can't tell if the weight of his arm around my shoulders helps or not. He's there for me. That's good. At least, that's what I tell the part of myself that wants the earth to swallow me. His arm gives me a squeeze. Pressure on the top of my head tells me he's kissed me. I push the corners of my mouth up, and my vision blurs. The quick wipe of my hand over my face does nothing except smear the fake smile. I destroy the contortion with a sharp sniff.

"Oh well." His voice is light. It floats somewhere above me, while my mind hovers in the twilight phase that always comes before one of my *moods*. "It just wasn't meant to be, I guess."

He repeats our new philosophy to me, the one we came up with to beat the depression, and kisses the top of my head again. I feel him breathe out into my hair. His warmth makes me feel cold.

"Sorry…"

The second the word comes out of my miserable mouth, he takes the laptop from my knees and sets it on the floor. I think he's turned the screen away from me on purpose. He's good like that.

Kneeling down, he shuffles forwards until my knees are hugging his hips. His arms wrap me up in that dark space against his chest. His heartbeat steadies my unstable breaths. The choking feeling doesn't ease, but it doesn't get any worse either.

"You have nothing to be sorry for, love."

My hiding place tightens around me, leaving less space for the scariness of the outside world. I mumble into the fluff of his old wool jumper,

"I hate disappointing you."

"Regi, you haven't. It's not the end of the world. You'll find something else, and we'll be fine. It'll all be fine, love. It's a rejection letter, not a death sentence."

"Feels like it is."

"Well, it's not. It just means this wasn't the job for you. The right one will come along soon."

His hand on the top of my head holds me in this safe little nook. The feel of his fingertips against my scalp makes me sleepy. I just want to sleep. Sleep and not wake up.

"I just… I feel… I feel like I'm… completely useless…"

"You're not useless, love."

"I am! I dropped ou-out of Uni, the depression and anxiety keep get-getting w-worse, and now I can't- can't even get a simple fucking job." My voice has broken but I don't care. My panic has caught me and suddenly I'm drowning in it. "I th-thought the in-interview went w-well! I th-thought they lie-liked me! I-I don't under-stand!"

I feel the warmth of his palms rub my back. Slow and steady, like soothing a baby. I suppose I am. Just one big baby.

"Regi." His voice is soft, but stern. "Stop it."

I sniff and speak to his jumper. I don't want to come out of the safe place he's built for me.

"S-stop what?"

"You know what."

"Ms Smith?"

I press my palms against my ears, but somehow her voice still breaks through.

"Ms Smith, we need you to come out of the cupboard now."

The shake in the nurse's voice makes the lava fume in the pit of my stomach. I can feel the anger rising out of it like smoke, and catching in my throat. Maybe it is smoke. It's definitely not bravery any more. I don't know if I'd ever have really called locking myself in a cupboard and refusing to come out brave.

"Miss Smith, this is pointless." The man, presumably the doctor who was appointed to put me down, tells me through the keyhole. "Your time is up. You can't hide in there forever so you might as well give up this little charade and come with us."

I don't know what makes it worse, the fact that I know he's right or the fact that he thinks I'm too dumb to realise it myself.

"Ms Smith, the police are coming. You really should come out. You really should."

I grit my teeth and press my hands harder against the sides of my head. Nails in the scalp. The nurse's voice sounds too much like I feel. Anyone would think she'd never had an objecting patient in her practice before. I take a minute to wonder if I'm really so bad at existing that I'm the only one who doesn't have the sense to roll over and die when they tell me to.

"Open the door, Miss Smith. Everything will be a lot easier if you do."

I run my hand over my face. It comes away wet, which rather settles the issue. They do not get to see me cry.

I'll be Schrödinger's cat: both alive and dead as long as I'm safe inside this dark little space. Only when there's nothing left to do but break it down will they find out that I'm already dead inside.

"Regi. Stop it."

"S-stop what?"

"You know what. Stop listening to them."

He means the voices. Not voices really. We've taken to characterising my depression and anxiety to help deal with them. They're easier to ignore if they're people: an 'Other' instead of a part of me. After four years of marriage he knows exactly when I'm listening to them.

"I can't help it."

I feel his arms shift around me, loosening. The darkness begins to brighten, but I cling to it, pressing my forehead against the sharp angle of his collarbone with a soft moan of objection. I hear his lungs puff. The little laugh stays hidden in his chest, but that doesn't mean I don't hear it. The next time I sniff some of the ash in my throat slips back down. It's a little easier to breathe.

"Come on," his voice says next to my ear, "I'll run you a bath."

I make another little moan, arms clinging around his middle.

"I'll put on some of the smelly candles."

He knows my weak spots too well. Another moan and a little grumble is all he's getting as a reply. His finger finds my cheek and strokes it. I don't want to smile, but for him I do. Eventually I nod too. Washing it off will help.

"Good."

The darkness recedes and far too soon the world outside his arms is real again.

❖ ❖ ❖

The whole struggle happens in a surreal silence. The door bursts open. The shelves flood with light, revealing the dust and dirt spread across the spray bottles and mop heads. My eyes only just glimpse the spiders fleeing before hands grab me and drag me into the light.

I can't breathe, but somehow I still smell the sterile scent of the doctor's surgery. My eyes are clouded with stinging tears, so when I hear the doctor tell me to just relax I can only make out the very edges of his face above me. He looks like a shadow.

Below my back is something hard. Inside, the sinking feeling has warped to a sunken one. I grip the rails on either side of me while my muscles fight: pull me up or hold me down. In the end, I think they do both.

"Don't worry. It'll be over soon."

I want to spit at him. I want to rage, and blast the boiling anger that's burning my chest into his face. But when I finally scream all that comes out is bubbles.

Ellis Sangster lives in the heart of the Scottish Highlands. She divides her time between studying History at the UHI, writing her novel with her co-author, Monica Burns (SF Caledonia), and correcting all the typos her cats make walking across the keyboarddddddddd.

SF Caledonia

Monica Burns

Colymbia
Robert Ellis Dudgeon
published 1873

This book feels like it should have been one of Gulliver's travels. The hero voyages away from Britain to start his adventure in a far-off land, when he is shipwrecked and cast adrift upon a strange ocean. Although, once he finds land, he is not tied down by tiny Lilliputians, he is greeted by a man dressed in bathing shorts, a pair of glasses and a police helmet, rising out of the water.

The majority of *Colymbia,* written in 1873 by Robert Ellis Dudgeon, is set beneath the waves of the Pacific Ocean. De Courcy Smith, the twenty-one year old protagonist, is taken in by the local people and introduced to their world. The land above them is almost uninhabitable, beneath a scorching sun and an active volcano, so the humans have taken to the coral reef surrounding the island, where they live permanently in an underwater civilisation named Colymbia. Like *Gulliver's Travels,* the book is about the discoveries and surprises to be found in a strange new civilisation, all the while satirising the writer's own contemporary civilisation. Those who have been keeping up with *SF Caledonia* will likely recognise this formula from books like *That Very Mab* (1885, Issue 7) and *Annals of the Twenty-Ninth Century* (1874, Issue 6). To this day in modern science fiction, the stranger in a strange land concept is used constantly, and for good reason. It allows the reader entry into this new world through a character who, like them, is also new to it, and so exploring the world is just as fascinating for both reader and protagonist (with any luck). I must tag on the usual disclaimer here, that *Colymbia* is a Victorian novel, and like many other novels explored in this series, and indeed from this century, it is often written more like an encyclopaedia of facts than a novel. Nowadays with our shorter attention spans and different demands and expectations from literature, this makes it less appealing than a modern SF book. However, as far as the Victorian novels we've explored in this series go, *Colymbia* is in my top three. Even while Dudgeon is, what we nowadays call 'info-dumping', his prose is entertaining, light and often funny. There is enough story progression and action to keep you interested. Importantly, there is enough substance to De Courcy as a character for the reader to care about him – far more so than a few of the others, such as Anados in *Phantastes* (Issue 5) and Diogenes Milton in *Annals of the Twenty Ninth Century* (Issue 6) or Maskull in *Voyage to Arcturus* (Issue 3) who function as little more than avatars through which to see the new world. Even his accounts of Colymbia are refracted through a strong personality, and his opinions and judgements say a lot about him.

De Courcy spends a great deal of time not just passively learning facts about Colymbia, but haughtily engaging in debate with the locals. A lot of their views contend with his firmly-held English values, which as readers, we know he holds dear from his declaration at the start of the novel: "I gained a profound conviction that this country was much superior to any country of ancient or modern times in both its political and social aspects." Very often, despite De Courcy's words of scorn about the Colymbians, you can feel that Dudgeon is mocking him and his values rather than the locals. He is a flawed but likeable character that you can believe as a real person. Often there are passages of psychological sensitivity – his survivor's guilt when he is shipwrecked, his wonder and confusion at the new society, his infatuation and heartbreak during a brief romantic entanglement, his homesickness for England, and then the poignancy and maladjustment he experiences once he's finally re-introduced to life on land.

If you are wondering how on earth De Courcy could talk to the Colymbians underwater, let alone breathe, Dudgeon is quick to explain. This is not a civilisation of merfolk – humans have not developed scales, tails or gills – it is purely by human ingenuity that people are able to survive under water. Dudgeon is always one step ahead of potential critics, eager to explain the inventions he has come up

Robert Ellis Dudgeon

with to enable life under the sea. Colymbian essentials are a canister of portable air, a weight belt to stop you rising to the surface, and a pair of counter-refraction glasses designed restore perfect vision under water. The portable air canister is not always needed because to breathe there is a vast network of air pipes across the city for free use. Dudgeon gives lengthy explanations of the intricacies of their construction. There are also reservoirs of air installed in many houses and public spaces where Colymbians can swim up and use the tanks of trapped air to talk normally. Otherwise, communication happens through a telegraphic language, done either through a series of gentle taps on the arm, or from a distance, clicking together two thimble-like instruments.

One of my favourite parts of reading the novels for *SF Caledonia* is finding those moments that are unintentionally far-seeing and relevant to our modern times, despite being written over a hundred years ago. This novel has a few clever satirical stabs at big corporations that really reflect our capitalist world today. Columbia has a lot of pushy big companies, such as those who supply the air tanks, and who literally charge you for the air you breathe.

One aspect I particularly liked was that Dudgeon foresees the use of tidal energy. He was not the first person to see the potential of tidal power, but reading this novel in the twenty-first century, when it is very important for the world to switch to clean, renewable energy, this quote is particularly prescient: "The irresistible power of the ocean's tides, as regular as clockwork and as inexhaustible as the ocean itself, acts with unfailing constancy, and without the noise, the smoke and the destructive effects of our steam-engines. The tides are nature's own motive power, which she offers to us without stint and free of expense. The Colymbians utilize the generous gift which we neglect for inferior forces that deafen us with their noise, ruin us with their costliness, and destroy us by their ill-regulated action."

De Courcy's conversations and debates with the locals are where the most enjoyable satire comes from. To appreciate it, the modern reader needs only general knowledge about Victorian values – enough to know that satirising things like the monarchy, religion, marriage and women's suffrage had the potential to ruffle a few feathers. Here are some examples to see what you make of them: Colymbian women wear trousers and only basic upper garments, and men wear only bathing shorts. They laugh out loud at De Courcy's stories of how Victorian people dress. In a debate with De Courcy, his friend Julian remarks, "Here everything is what it seems – our hair and our complexions, our limbs and our other organs, are all our own. Every one is as the hand of nature has fashioned him or her. I can imagine a couple of terrestrials being entrapped into mutual admiration by the beautifying arts of your tailors, milliners, hair-dressers and dealers in cosmetics. And when they got married they would find to their chagrin, that it was not one another they admired, but only clothes and wigs, padding, rouge and powder!"

Colymbia is ruled by a government, but they also have a monarch. The King of Colymbia is a sea turtle, highly pampered, attended by servants and bedecked in fine jewellery, and he serves no purpose other than to be a decorative figurehead at ceremonies. Colymbian religion consists of "transcendental geography", which is belief in a superior race of "unknown people" who live in a place that they don't know whether or not actually exists. People try to emulate the imagined behaviours of these unknown people in order to be better people themselves.

Colymbian women don't work, but there is a huge movement in society to get them to work – except not by the women themselves, but by the men. Women don't *want* to work, but the men are pleading with them to do their fair share of society's heavy lifting. I for one, hope that this is Dudgeon laughing at his own society's misogynists rather than at the suffrage movement. There are little comments here and there throughout the book that give me hope that Dudgeon might be on the feminists' side. When it is explained to De Courcy that women are condemned far more harshly than men for small things in Colymbia, De Courcy points out, "How very droll […] that what is a trivial error in the one sex should be a mortal sin in the other."

All this, to me as a modern and liberal person, is delightfully funny and sounds very progressive, particularly when reading a reviewer, writing in March 1873 in *The Saturday Review of Politics, Literature, Science and Art*, getting indignant at the idea that this book might be "a highly immoral publication" and has to argue his way to convince himself and his readers that it is not. As a modern reader, I *wish* it was a highly immoral publication, and that Dudgeon meant exactly what I hoped he did by his satire. But there is a danger, as a modern and liberal person, of projecting my own values onto this 19th century book. The *Saturday Review* journalist also had this to say: "The writer, like all other designers of a new Utopia, has of course a moral to convey; though we must confess that we are not always very clear as to the precise point of his preachings" and that "The fable necessarily admits of more than one interpretation, and it is always possible that the writer may be laughing at us in his sleeve." To a modern reader, this is a good thing. You want your writer to problematise and draw attention to things so you can think for yourself – nobody likes "preachings". Not knowing the target of satire makes you think critically of all sides – the Colymbians, De Courcy himself and the society he was born and raised in. You could tie yourself in knots trying to work out who Dudgeon is really laughing at. It is part of what makes the book so entertaining.

The first thing I wanted to know about Robert Ellis Dudgeon was whether he had done any practical research for *Colymbia*. It turns out he was a keen swimmer and published a book called *The Swimming Baths of London* in 1870 (three years before *Colymbia*) the first line of which is, "swimming is an exercise at once healthful, pleasant and useful". From the amount of detail in *Colymbia*, this was expected, but I was amazed to find out that Dudgeon also actually invented a pair of underwater counter-refraction glasses as he describes in his novel. He wrote a book on his studies called *The Human Eye*. Despite his many publications, *Colymbia* is Dudgeon's only work of fiction. He wrote it as a response to another utopian novel, *Erewhon*, published the previous year, which was written by his friend and patient Samuel Butler.

Dudgeon's background is not in literature but medicine and homeopathy. And in his field Dudgeon was very eminent, not just at home, but internationally. Born to a well-off merchant family in Leith in 1820 and privately educated, Dudgeon attended the University of Edinburgh to train as a doctor. He practiced in Liverpool and London, became particularly interested in homeopathy, and pursued that as his life's work. Not only did he lecture and publish widely in his field, he was also elevated to several prominent positions at various points in his life: secretary, vice-president then president of the British Homeopathic Society, president of the International Homeopathic Congress, and the editor of the British Journal of Homeopathy.

Homeopathy did not enjoy a good reputation in Dudgeon's time, and since then it has been dubbed, at best, as alternative medicine, but mostly dismissed as a pseudoscience. Despite what one might think of his career in homeopathy, Dudgeon was also very accomplished in medical research. He wrote extensively on vision and the eye, and the underwater spectacles were not the only thing he invented. Some may recognise his name from what became known as the 'Dudgeon's Sphygmograph'. The sphygmograph was a mechanical instrument that recorded the force, rate and variations in the pulse – the 19th century predecessor of the modern arm cuffs used to measure blood pressure. Although it wasn't initially Dudgeon's invention, he revolutionised it by improving on the design, reducing its size and making it portable by a strap on the wrist. On this account, his version of the sphygmograph became the most popular in Britain. Long after Dudgeon died, in 1904 after a spell of bad health, his name lives on predominantly through his invention. There are many 'Dudgeon's Sphygmographs' in museums today, including the Science Museum, London.

Monica Burns is the Assistant Editor and First Reader at *Shoreline of Infinity*. She is also a writer – co-authors with Ellis Sangster (*The Useless Citizen Act*) – comics artist and perpetual student. She has just finished her second Masters degree at her third Scottish university.

Art: Mark Toner

Colymbia

(extract)

Robert Ellis Dudgeon

CHAPTER VI.

SHARK-HUNTING.

UNDER the guidance of Julian, I was gradually initiated into all the sports and pastimes of the Colymbians. In some of these the ladies take part; but there is one sport of too violent and dangerous a character for women to engage in, so it is pursued by men only. It demands such agility, address and courage, that it is only the most adventurous and daring among the young men who engage in it. When I mention that it is the pursuit of the formidable white shark, the reader will understand that it must be attended by difficulties and dangers which all but the boldest would shrink from.

In remote times, as I was informed, these finny ogres of the ocean were not unfrequent visitors of the calm inland waters, to which they gained access by numerous gaps in the surrounding coral reef. But all these gaps had long ago been filled up, and the reef rendered a perfect barrier against the incursions of these ferocious monsters.

As the numbers of the inhabitants increased the original boundaries of the reef were greatly extended by the planting of corals outside the existing reef, which rapidly grew up. In place of a separate reef for each island, one larger reef was thus made, which enclosed all the islands. There are about a dozen islands in all, of different sizes. The largest is about sixty miles in length by about fifteen in breadth, and the remainder range from twenty miles to half a mile in diameter. By this means many hundreds of square miles have been gradually added to the space suitable for human habitation. These new spaces were all amply supplied with air-tubes and electric lamps. The old barriers that had separately surrounded each island were removed, and the additional space was rapidly covered with submarine houses and villas, thus providing accommodation for the ever increasing population. The new reef quickly rose above the level of the highest tides, opposing a perfect barrier against the inroads of the sea. But as it was requisite to secure a continuous flow of fresh water through the enclosed lake, the reef was perforated with tunnels in every direction, which, by means of a system of self-acting valvular doors, permitted the influx and efflux of the ocean currents in a gentle and equable manner. In order to maintain the water of the inland sea at a uniform temperature, these tunnels were pierced at different levels. The water of the ocean near the surface is of a much higher temperature than the deeper water; and when the enclosed water becomes too warm the fresh water is admitted chiefly by the lower tunnels; when it is too cool the influx through the more superficial tunnels soon raises it to the required temperature. By self-acting machinery the upper valves open as the temperature lowers, the lower as the temperature rises. Special inspectors and engineers are appointed to maintain the tunnels and doors in perfect efficiency, and to see that the enclosed water keeps at a uniform temperature. So well are their duties performed that while the enclosed water is always sweet and clear, its temperature never varies above a degree or two, and the flow through the lake is so gentle and so regular that it can scarcely be perceived, and it is hardly strong enough to bend the slender-stemmed seaweeds that adorn the submarine country and give such a charm to the open spaces between the houses.

As the mighty game which was to be attacked no longer existed in the inland sea, it had to be sought beyond the coral barrier, and great preparations had to be made for its pursuit.

On the occasion of my first shark-hunting expedition, to which Julian introduced me, our party consisted of ten young men in the prime of life and strength. We were accompanied by two regular huntsmen, one of whom was a tough old salt who had held the situation for upwards of twenty years, and was believed to be thoroughly conversant with all the ways and wiles of the great white shark, many hundreds of which he had assisted to kill and capture. The other was a younger man, who had assisted the chief huntsmen in many of his perilous expeditions, and who was considered to be scarcely inferior to his elder mate in skill and coolness.

As we should have to quit the region of air-tubes, we were all provided with a metal bottle of compressed oxygenated air, which was suspended by a strap round our necks, and provided with a tube to which we could readily apply our lips when we needed a breath of air.

Each of us carried in his hand a short wooden spear about three feet in length, having at the end a sharp steel point about ten inches long.

The two huntsmen did not carry spears, but each had an instrument formed of a stout iron rod, about eighteen inches in length, armed at both ends with several sharp barbed points springing from a thick knob. They had also a harpoon, to the handle of which was attached a cord, which had at its free end an apparatus which opened out like a small umbrella when the cord was dragged rapidly through the water, presenting a large surface that opposed considerable resistance to the water.

The air-bottles and spears we carried being made so as to have the same specific gravity as the water did not affect our position in it; but the iron weapons of the huntsmen being so much heavier than water would have sunk their bearers, had they not restored their equipoise by inflating some of the cells of their weight-belts.

Near the coral barrier was a large cage containing a fine pack of lively pilot-fish, each about a foot long, their beautiful grey body encircled by several bands of bright blue. The huntsmen opened the door of the cage and allowed about a score to issue forth. They seemed to understand what they were wanted for, and frisked and gambolled round and about our party just like little dogs, evidently delighted at the prospect of the hunt.

These little fish, as is well known to naturalists, feel a strange attraction for the white shark, and are constantly seen in his company. Unlike other fish they have no fear of the fierce monster, but will pursue him wherever he goes, darting at his eyes, body and fins, and even approaching so near his mouth as to make it difficult to understand how they escape certain death from his lancet-shaped teeth, unless the shark entertains a friendly feeling for them.

This propensity of the pilot-fish has been utilized by the Colymbians, who train packs of them in order to scent out the quarry and guide the bold hunters to their huge game.

White sharks in these regions attain to a prodigious size. Specimens have been killed nearly forty feet long, with such capacious mouths that it would be easy for them to swallow a man at one gulp.

Raising the door that closed one of the tunnels, we all, including the pilot-fishes, which danced merrily before us, passed through the tunnel and emerged into the ocean beyond.

The appearance of the water beyond the barrier is quite different to what it is within the reef. There, as I have said, it is not very deep, and the bottom is composed of corals, astræas, madrepores, and seaweeds. But beyond the barrier at this point we came almost at once into water so deep that no bottom could be seen, and we looked down into a dark blue void which reflected no light from its depths. The appearance looking upward was also quite different. There was the circular opening with its thin prismatic border through which the sky was visible and any seafowl that might be flying overhead, but beyond the circular opening all was like a dark mirror, reflecting nothing but the white bodies of those of our party who were at a little distance from me.

As soon as we had gained the open sea, the pilot-fish left off their gambols and set themselves seriously to their work. They kept pretty close together and proceeded to hunt the water like well-trained pointers. We let them go some fifty yards in advance, and, preserving that distance between us, carefully watched their movements. For a considerable time they went wheeling about in every direction, always keeping well together, and moving to right or left as if all animated by one impulse.

All at once they left off wheeling about, and moved steadily forward in one direction, but so slowly and cautiously that they hardly seemed to move a fin.

The old huntsman, who was close to me, and under whose special charge I was advised to place myself, tapped on my arm: "He is not far off."

Advancing cautiously after our finny guides, it was not long before we perceived the dim outline of a gigantic shark suspended motionless in the water.

I confess to having experienced a most uncomfortable sensation as our diminishing distance revealed the stupendous proportions of this tiger of the sea.

The plucky little pack of pilot-fishes were soon alongside of him, and quitting their close formation, they distributed themselves on all sides of the unsuspecting brute. They darted at his head, his body, his fins, and especially at his eyes. Their vivacious attacks seemed rather to please the shark, who only showed signs of life by a slight quiver of his dorsal fin, or a languid movement of his dull but wicked-looking eye.

While the attention of the monster was thus occupied by his tiny teazers, the younger huntsman had crept up cautiously behind and beneath him, and on getting within a convenient distance he launched his harpoon at the fish's belly with such a sure aim that it buried itself over its projecting barbs in his body. At the same instant the previous apathy of the animal was changed to the wildest and most excited action. With vigorous strokes of his powerful tail he darted rapidly forwards. The little-pilot fish scampered off in every direction, and we followed as fast as we could the retreating form of the wounded, but still powerful creature. The umbrella-like appendage to the harpoon opening up offered a considerable obstacle to the shark's progress through the water, so that we were enabled to keep him well in sight. Our pack of pilot-fish, aware that their services were not required in the present state of matters, formed into a close phalanx and kept behind us. The pain of the harpoon or the obstruction caused by its drag soon caused the shark to relax the speed of his pace and enabled us to come to close quarters.

At once, he seemed to resolve no longer to fly from his tormentors, but, turning rapidly, he rushed boldly among us, his eyes glaring at us with a malignant expression of fishy ferocity. With much address, the hunters avoided his onslaught, and as he darted through their ranks, they dodged on one side, and several well-directed thrusts of their sharp spears added to the fury of the animal. As it passed the old huntsman, he dexterously planted his harpoon in the shark's flank, which doubled the obstacle to his passage through the water. Slowly turning, he again made for his enemies, who scattered to either side as before, all but the old huntsman, who rather threw himself in the direct line of the now slowly moving fish. He was slightly above the shark's level, and as the monster came beneath him, it suddenly turned round, belly upwards, opening its awful jaws, armed with a triple row of sharpest teeth. I was horror-struck, thinking it was all over with the gallant old huntsman. But I did not know his resources. Unawed by the gaping cavity that was opened to engulf him, the old hero thrust his hand, in which he held the iron weapon before described, deep into the creature's mouth. The jaws were suddenly approximated, but the pronged and barbed iron instrument, sticking into the flesh above and below, kept them from shutting, and the baffled monster lashed about him in impotent fury, "Now, boys, close in upon him!" signed the sturdy veteran, and we all rushed at the enfeebled creature with a will. A dozen spears were plunged into his bleeding flanks, quickly withdrawn, and plunged in again and again, and in a few moments this thing of terror lay a lifeless corpse in the blood-stained water. We measured him as he lay, and found that his length from snout to tip of tail was just thirty-one feet four inches. His gaping mouth had a triple row of sharp flat teeth, lying inclined towards his throat, rendering it impossible for any living thing that had once got into his capacious mouth to be withdrawn or ejected.

I asked the huntsman how we were to transport our magnificent bag to the reef. "Well," he said, "had we been farther from the reef, we should have had to drag him back as best we might. But as we are only about half a mile from home we need not be put to that trouble. Here, Jack!" he signalled to his companion, "go and whistle for the seals."

Jack immediately began to mount to the surface, and I accompanied him, anxious to see what was coming next. On our heads rising above the surface of the water, we could just see the top of the reef, where several persons seemed to be on the outlook for us. Jack blew a shrill whistle on his fingers, whereupon a man, who was evidently watching for the signal, slipped the chain off the necks of two of the watch seals which lay beside him. These animals immediately flopped into the water and disappeared. In a few minutes their round bullet heads popped up beside us, and their large, intelligent-looking but flattish eye seemed to say, "Here we are; what do you wish us to do?" Jack patted them on the crown, and pointing down below, descended head-foremost. The seals and I quickly followed, and we were soon beside the rest of the company, who were waiting for our arrival. The harpoon-cords, which still hung from the shark's body, were fastened to the collars the seals wore, and they immediately set off with their heavy burden at a pretty good pace.

As the big body moved off, the little pilot-fish frisked around it as if in the exuberance of delight at the visible result of the day's hunt. The huntsmen went along with the seals to assist in getting the shark into the inhabited sea.

The sportsmen followed at their leisure discussing the events of the chase, and disputing with one another as to the relative size, strength and ferocity of this compared with other sharks they had hunted. One of the party produced a bottle filled with compressed exhilarating gas, which was passed from hand to hand, and increased our gaiety.

In this way we gained the enclosed sea, where we found a large number of ladies and gentlemen assembled to meet and congratulate us on our success. None of our party had been injured by the shark, if I except a smart smack on the back one of them had received from a whisk of his tail. I was told that accidents seldom happened, for though the shark looked so fierce and formidable, it was, on the whole, a stupid creature, and the awkward position of its mouth on the under surface of the head, rendering it always necessary for it to turn round on its back before it could bite at anything above it, always allowed a tolerably agile person to elude its snap. Legs and arms had occasionally been lost by inhabitants of Colymbia, but such accidents rarely, if ever, occurred to the hunters. The victims were almost invariably unarmed turtle-hunters or pearl-fishers, whom the sharks caught unawares.

The body of the shark, which was the perquisite of the professional huntsmen, was sold by them to the butchers. The flesh, though coarse and strong flavoured, finds a ready sale among the poorer people, and the skin is in great request for professors' collars, for straps and book-covers.

During my stay in Colymbia, I frequently enjoyed the exciting sport of shark-hunting. Sometimes we would fail to find a fish; sometimes the game, after being wounded, would make his escape, with a harpoon sticking in his body; sometimes we were so fortunate as to meet with two in company, both of which we would bag; and, sometimes, we would capture a brace or two of turtle, which we would bring home alive. But I need not detail the incidents of other shark-hunts, as I have so much more to say about other features of life in Colymbia.

THE BEACHCOMBER PRESENTS

Where Have All The Time Machines Gone?

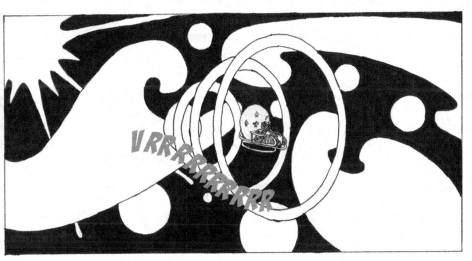

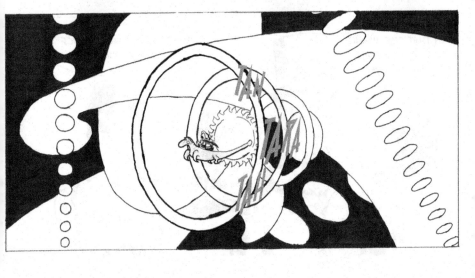

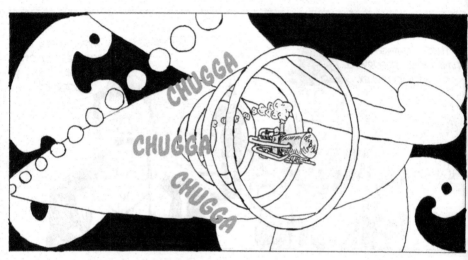

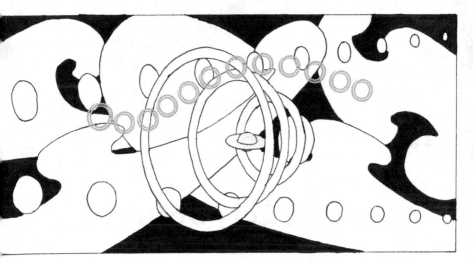

Interview: Cory Doctorow

Cory Doctorow (craphound.com) is a science fiction author, activist and journalist – the co-editor of *Boing Boing* (boingboing. net) and the author of many books, most recently *Walkaway*. Born in Toronto, Canada, Cory Doctorow now lives in Los Angeles.

Here he is in conversation with **Joanna McLaughlin** for *Shoreline of Infinity*.

JM: In your new novel, a group of people literally 'walk away' from a corrupt, exploitative society in the near future and in doing so, challenge existing systems and beliefs about what's needed and valued in life. When you were writing *Walkaway*, did you imagine the new society that the characters created as one that could really exist in our world? Would it be a society you would want to live in?

CD: *Walkaway* is people dealing gracefully with a crisis, and I'd obviously prefer that we just didn't have a crisis. However, just planning not to have a crisis is no way to prevent one. People who design systems on the assumption that a crisis will never arise, don't build great things, they build the Titanic. Of all the ways that we could deal with a crisis, the *Walkaway* way is not a terrible one – it's people rising to the occasion, figuring stuff out and generally being kind to each other, even when they can't agree about everything. And when they do find places where they have irreconcilable differences, they have relatively peaceful ways of resolving them. So that feels like it isn't a terrible way to approach the future.

In terms of whether it's plausible, I'm not trying to predict anything. Science fiction writers are not great predictors, which is good because if the future was predictable it would arrive no matter what we did and there would be no reason to even get out of bed in the morning. But I think what science fiction writers can do is to inspire and to warn – we can help people think about different ways of approaching the problems that are coming. So while I don't necessarily think we will get a world like *Walkaway*, using *Walkaway* as a landmark on the horizon to move towards an uncertain and shifting terrain might get us somewhere interesting. All people and places fall short of their ideals and some people fall short of better ideals than others.

JM: So perhaps *Walkaway* isn't necessarily the alternative society that we should try to create, but it helps us realise that there are alternatives out there. *Walkaway* is set in a post-scarcity society, where 3D printers are readily used

to create a wide range of resources and help create a fairer society where property isn't just in the hands of the few. It's exciting to think how technological advancements can help tackle some of the challenges the world faces as resources start to run out.

CD: In the book 3D printing is as much metaphor as it is explanation. With or without 3D printing, we now have significantly more efficient manufacturing than we've ever had. There are super-efficient supply chains, super-efficient factories, brilliant tool and dye makers, super exploitative labour relations, the ability to externalise the cost of diesel and carbon in long haul shipping. It's all this stuff in concert that delivers this output. 3D printing is a nice way to think about that in a manageable way that you can get your arms around, rather than technology's big spider web of economical and social arrangements.

However, the reality is that even without 3D printing, the objects that we own are much more fluid and require significantly less labour, material and energy than objects people owned a generation ago. The things that stay in an Ikea catalogue year after year are the things that get lighter and lighter every year. The manufacturers are figuring out how to make things of the same strength but with less material, and they pack into less space every year so that the shipped cubic footage continuously goes down. You don't need a 3D printer to have manufacturing miracles all around you all the time.

JM: Unlike many science fiction novels, I like that *Walkaway* doesn't just focus on people surviving in a dystopian society, but shows them coming together to create a better society. Why did you decide to go down that route with this novel?

CD: I think science fiction's great strength is that it is a pulp literature, which means it foregrounds plotting over everything else. When you're doing that, you get to get away with calling on the reader to exercise willing suspension of disbelief while you draw something that is manifestly unrealistic, to allow the plot to go forward. That's why it's often the case that someone's mobile phone packs in at just the moment they need to convey some urgent message, so they have to race across town under great pressure.

In disaster novels we like to sideline the reality of what happens in disasters, which is that people are generally magnificent and rise to the occasion in a moment when all the pettiness of life falls away. When you're writing a disaster novel you generally sideline that and turn it into a man against nature against man story where, when something bad goes down, your neighbours come over to eat you because that's more exciting than just a man against man or a man against nature story.

However, one of the things I've discovered is when you take the thing that we normally set aside to service the plot and actually make the plot fit within its constraints, this creates an immediacy and a veracity that makes readers really engage with the material. So, writing a novel where there is a crisis and people are rising magnificently to the occasion – but not necessarily able to agree with each other about what should be done – you're increasing the drama, because instead of imagining the conflict arising because of enmity with your enemies, it shows the conflict arising because of irreconcilable differences you have with your friends. By focussing on a semi-realistic response to disaster, and therefore people trying to make a better world and recover instead of turning into 'Mad Max cannibals', I think I

was able to create a world that readers can really engage with.

JM: And as you say, I suppose part of a realistic response to a crisis, is that even though people agree that change is needed they don't necessarily agree what that change should look like. In *Walkaway*, we see the main characters debate different philosophical, political viewpoints at length (e.g. meritocracy versus equalitarianism). Did you deliberately set out to give space to different views?

CD: It's a long tradition to have science fiction play out different philosophical debates, with a lot of what we consider science fiction arising from philosophical thought experimentation. If people are willing to read 15 pages of JK Rowling describing how magic works because what she writes is interesting (even if magic doesn't really exist), then I think they are also willing to engage with interesting material that has some immediacy and relates to real issues in the world that they are dealing with. This is particularly true when this material is built into

"I think what science fiction writers can do is to inspire and to warn"

an exciting action story and, in turn, it makes this action more consequential because you can see why people are doing what they're doing.

If you have to spend a lot of resources to bring a group together, and you need it to stay together for a long time, then you'll dedicate a lot of time to making sure you're all there for the same reason. However, when group forming is cheap – like it is now with social media – it doesn't matter if everyone is doing it for exactly the same reason or if sometime down the road you can't work together anymore, because it took so little resource to set up and whatever it achieves is a net benefit. One of the things I was trying to engage with in *Walkaway* is what an ad-hoc activist network might look like as a more institutionalised group that carries on for many years, rather than just dissolving when its initial project is over.

JM: I was really conscious that the end of *Walkaway* felt like it could segue into one of your earlier novels, *Down and Out in the Magic Kingdom*. Do you have a sense of your novels existing on the same timeline?

CD: My novels are explicitly not on a timeline and I always try not to peg a year in my books, as I think it makes them atemporal and therefore a little more evergreen. I will often deliberately add anachronistic elements to confound your ability to peg an actual date onto them. Somewhere between 10 minutes and 100 years in the future is generally where I'm shooting for in most of my books.

However, without trying to be continuous, or in any way make *Walkaway* a direct prequel to *Down and Out in the Magic Kingdom,* I did try to imagine what an intermediate state between today and *Down and Out in the Magic Kingdom* might look like. But I gave myself the leeway not to have to make the years line up.

I took my inspiration from a great writer, mostly known for his short stories, called John Burley. He wrote all these beautiful, brilliant stories that were linked thematically and even shared characters and settings, but didn't share a timeline. So his stories took on an almost mythic quality, where sometimes they reference each other but sometimes they don't. That was kind of the zone I was shooting for with *Walkaway*, where if you'd read *Down and Out in the Magic Kingdom* it would inform your understanding and be in dialogue with the book, without it being a literal prequel.

JM: Finally, a lot of *Shoreline of Infinity*'s readers are aspiring writers – do you have any tips for people writing science fiction stories?

I think that when we start writing, we write often for heroic reasons because we're inspired. The thing about inspiration is that it's out of your control and you can't muster it on demand, so you need to learn to also write when you're not inspired. Generally, the feeling that the words you're writing are no good is just as untrue as the feeling the words you're writing are brilliant. On average, the words that you write will be about average, so even on days when you think your words are terrible, you just need to write them. Six months later you won't be able to tell the difference between your brilliant words and your so-called terrible words, and you'll realise that they're all just about average for you, and then you can fix them. And the way you fix them is by focussing on your weaknesses not your strengths. It feels really good to polish the parts that you've already done a good job with because you're directing your attention to something that you can feel proud of, but to focus on the stuff that you struggle with is to give yourself the chance for some really significant improvement. So to go from 95% to 96% is nothing but to go from 10% to 50% is amazing, and will make you a much better writer.

Another tip is to write every day. Pick a word target: to write 1 page or 2 pages, 20 minutes or half an hours writing. Finish half way through a sentence so you have somewhere to pick up the next day without having to be creative. Imagine your character is a person, in a place with a problem who is trying intelligently to solve it, and failing, which gives them a new problem to solve. Make sure they fail through no fault of their own, so the reader continues to sympathise with them. Eventually if you keep doing that long enough, the problem will get so intense that there's no way it can get worse and that's the climax, and then your story is over. Remember that confusion is not the same as suspense and that unless you have a damn good reason not to, tell the reader exactly what is going on and not just hint at it. The action in the story comes from knowing what's going on, not just trying to figure out what's going on. That's my advice!

Joanna McLaughlin works with local government in Scotland. She is a fan of all things science fiction and springer spaniel.

Reviews

Shattered Minds
Laura Lam
Tor, 400 pages
Review by Eris Young

In a future North American West Coast ruled behind the scenes by a sinister corporation called Sudice, neurological experiments are conducted on criminals and drug addicts: people the company think no one will miss. One of these addicts is Carina, a neuroprogrammer and former Sudice employee whose dark past and violent urges have increasingly forced her to escape into a drug-induced virtual reality.

When a former colleague contacts Carina with encrypted evidence that could lead to Sudice's downfall, Carina has no choice but to team up with a group of hackers and try to bring down the company that destroyed her life. It is her work with these hackers that will eventually help her start to heal, but will the danger Carina poses to others prove too great?

Laura Lam's *Shattered Minds* is a cleverly imagined piece of cyberpunk fiction that renders a startling future in intimate but bleak detail. The world of *Shattered Minds* is one where the omnipresence of technology gives rise to moral complications and social dynamics that would never occur to to most of us today. For example, the rich and famous of Pacifica cover themselves completely, for fear of being cloned from a stray piece of DNA, and 'school' consists merely of downloading information directly into students' brains.

Lam fully integrates technology into the plot as well: throughout *Shattered Minds* technology seems to create as many problems as it solves, forcing the protagonists into less a game of cat-and-mouse than an outright cold war, in which the side with better tech wins.

The most interesting aspect of Lam's world-building was

the way she talks about mind, memory and dreams: as data to be analysed, stored, recorded and overwritten. The idea that human minds and personalities could be so well integrated with external data systems that they are expandable and, more importantly, mutable, is deeply unsettling.

Lam plays with the idea of thought-as-data deftly and deeply, and takes it as far as it will go: with the technology available to Sudice and the world at large, what's to stop someone rewriting another person's entire personality, or even one's own? This was the story's most powerful dimension.

The cast of characters in *Shattered Minds* is also as diverse as should be expected from a book set in the far future, most notable in the character of Dax, a transgender man who was born and raised in the North American Shoshone tribe.

I readily admit that I tend to approach books featuring transgender characters (almost always written by cisgender authors) with more trepidation than excitement. I was unsure how Dax's character would be drawn and I was afraid he'd fall victim to one of the many, nearly always tragic, stereotypes of a trans character.

But I found Dax to be intricately and sensitively drawn, and was relieved to see that while his gender identity – actualised that much more easily in a world where body modification is the norm – informs his personality, history and interactions with the other characters, it is not the be-all end-all of his personhood. Dax is a multi-dimensional character with a complex relationship to the other

SHATTERED MINDS | LAURA LAM

protagonists, especially Carina, that contributes substantially to both the plot and Carina's development.

I'm less sure (and less qualified to talk about) how Dax's Native-Americanness plays into his character. I did at times feel that it was a bit extraneous, a box ticked in the name of diversity. However there's a fine line between richness of character and outright stereotype, and Lam walks this line delicately. Anyway, why should Dax not be Native? White is not – and should not be – default. It's reasonable for Dax to be Native American, but it's also reasonable that Lam point it out explicitly. After all we don't live in a world where a reader is likely to assume a character is Native American if it's not mentioned outright. In Dax, Lam is representing one of a number of cultural groups who are easily elided; Indigenous cultures are often assumed to be 'archaic' or even extinct, so to see Shoshone culture represented in a sci-fi novel, in however small a way, strikes a distinctly hopeful note.

The concepts in *Shattered Minds* are inventive and convincing. Lam has created, in Pacifica, a startlingly believable extrapolation of our current world, in which technology is increasingly integrated into everyday life. In doing so, she questions the true nature of the qualities that make us human.

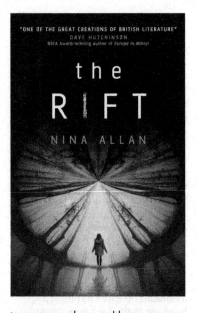

The Rift
Nina Allan
Titan Books, 400 pages
Review by Neil Williamson

The very simple truth at the heart of Nina Allan's brilliant new novel is that between any two people there exists a chasm. No matter how close someone is to you – friends, lovers, family – no matter how completely you trust them, you can never know 100% that the things they tell you are true. In the end you can only choose to believe them, or not.

In *The Rift*, a teenager named Julie Rouane goes missing in 1994 in the vicinity of a local lake. The awful mundanities of an extensive police search are played out and, despite two separate and ultimately futile arrests, Julie's fate is never discovered. Her family do their best to move on. Twenty years later, Julie's younger sister, Selena, is contacted by a woman who claims to be Julie. She's the right age, she looks similar and she knows things only Julie would know, and in her heart Selena knows that this really is the sister she has thought dead her entire adult life. But she can't quite make herself believe it.

Such a set-up may be familiar to genre readers, and how you choose to interpret it may depend on your genre of choice. Crime readers might suspect murder and imposture, supernatural horror fans might think they're seeing a ghost, and science fiction aficionados would be forgiven for going straight to the drawer marked alien abduction. And the brilliance of the way the story unfolds is any of these interpretations could be true, it just depends on which of the apparently conflicting elements you choose to believe.

In the second part of the book, Julie tells her own story. She wasn't abducted, she claims. Not really. Instead, she stumbled through a portal – a rift – into another world, a planet called Tristane. There she lived with a brother and sister, Cally and Noah, until she found her way back again. Julie's detailed account of Tristane is built on a surfeit of facts that make it seem every bit as believable as our own world and, if invented, would entail a prodigious feat of imagination. And, as we read on, we come to question some of the facts we've learned about our own world too. The story is carefully littered with found documents that contribute veracity to this interpretation or undermine that. Julie's high school essay on the book and film, *Picnic At Hanging Rock*, is an especially poignant touchstone.

By the end of *The Rift*, we and Selena are in the same position. The book is so well balanced, so intricately constructed that, knowing everything that we know, we still don't have a definitive truth. But do we need it? If you want it to be a science fiction story of reconciliation, it is. If you want it to be a story of dangerous delusion, it can be that too.

What is in no doubt is that Nina Allan's *The Rift* is a high class piece of fiction and a triumph of storytelling.

Sirens
Simon Messingham
Derelict Space Sheep, 338 pages
Review by Katie Gray

I was tentatively excited for *Sirens*. Being a die-hard *Doctor Who* fan I was familiar with Simon Messingham's work – he's the author of no less than seven expanded universe novels across four different books ranges. Naturally I was interested to read his first original novel and *Sirens* had an intriguing and gripping premise.

All around the world, two hundred people simultaneously acquire the same superpower: the ability to 'glamour' other human beings, to make them fall utterly and wholeheartedly in love with you. Glamoured people will do anything their new master asks of them – even at the cost of their own lives.

One of the newly made Sirens is Anthony Graves, a thirty-year-old London office worker. He was wholly unimaginative and unremarkable. Now he rules all of Europe and North America – and he has designs on the rest of the world. The narrative switches between his aimless life of luxury and extended flashbacks detailing how he came to realise what he could do, how he came to be emperor, and what he lost along the way.

Sirens doesn't get too bogged down in how and why the eponymous beings exist. They simply *do*, and the consequences are dealt with in a realistic way, the destruction and subsequent reorganisation of society made to feel chillingly real.

SIRENS

SIMON
MESSINGHAM

Messingham has a real flair for the disturbing. *Sirens* is an often skin-crawling read, in large part due to the strength of the world-building – it's clear a lot of thought has been put into exactly what two hundred, randomly selected people having this power would *mean*. An infant Siren destroys an entire town in its panic; an elderly woman with dementia first kills the other patients in her care home and then incinerates half of Europe.

Ther are some fascinating concepts in *Sirens*. What really lets the novel down is its protagonist; every other Siren seems to have a more interesting story than Anthony Graves.

Some of the new Sirens try to use their abilities for good, some for evil and destruction. Others reject their new existence altogether and choose to take their own lives. Anthony does none of the above.

At no point does it occur to Anthony to make a conscious moral choice about how to use his power, for good and for evil. He uses the Glamour to have fun and ensure his continued existence. He isn't even imaginative enough to think of anything to *do* with his power – he has to be prompted by others to realise that he can get anything more ambitious than free drinks in bars. Even when he glamours all of Britain, it's because someone else pulled some strings to get him a TV interview.

He's shown to be deeply sexist and homophobic, and he struggles to connect with other people, especially women. All of this informs the way he uses his ability; selfishly, pettily, and violently. One way or another, he kills every woman he has a sexual relationship with.

We've all known men like Anthony, nasty, immature creeps and it's all too plausible that given this kind of power, they would snap and become killers. But the novel presents Anthony as a kind of everyman, or even an every*person*; the message of the novel could easily be taken as that in Anthony's circumstances, we would all become not just monsters but petty monsters.

But on the flip side, it's worth noting that the handful of Sirens indicated to have chosen death over dominating others are all women, which I can only assume was intentional. *Sirens* could also be understood as a commentary on sexism and male entitlement.

Late in the novel, Anthony realises he's come across as a villain. He claims he hasn't been doing himself justice in his own autobiography (the book we're reading) and that he did all sorts of interesting and creative things with his power. But he then struggles to name any of them or even to tell the reader anything 'true' and authentic about himself.

Sirens is certainly a thought-provoking book. Ultimately, though, I think Messingham is more concerned with being dark and 'edgy' than with communicating a coherent moral message. Was *Sirens* intended to be about misogyny, or about human nature? Both interpretations are supported by the text and neither is fully satisfying.

I enjoyed reading *Sirens*, but I think perhaps it might have been stronger as an ensemble piece, with several different Sirens sharing the spotlight. As it is, the more I reflect on it, the more I dislike it.

Under the Pendulum Sun
Jeannette Ng
Angry Robot, 416 pages
Review by Marija Smits

The central premise of *Under the Pendulum Sun* is a strong one: to what lengths will a missionary go to bring faith to the faithless? But here's where the premise gets really interesting – the faithless are the inhabitants of Arcadia, the fae.

Laon Helstone is the Victorian missionary in question, and yet the story is told from the viewpoint of his sister, Catherine. It is Catherine who goes in search of him when his letters from Arcadia suddenly stop arriving, and it is Catherine who reveals to us the wonders, perplexities and mysteries of Arcadia as she first sets foot in the world of the fae.

Under the Pendulum Sun very obviously draws from classics such as *Jane Eyre* as well as the literary works of the Romantic poets. Indeed, the heroine, Catherine is somewhat like Jane, though she is not nearly as likeable (or morally upstanding). There is also the influence of the more modern depictions of the fae (I'm thinking particularly of Susannah Clarke's excellent *Jonathan Strange and Mr Norrell* and though perhaps unknowingly, the similar-in-tone *The Spider's Bride* by Debbie Gallagher).

Ng draws us into the fantastic quickly, with gorgeously imaginative details. I particularly liked the idea of the sea whale – a whale that ploughs through the earth and contains the sea within it, as well as the semiotic moths who ingest words. A real Goblin Market was a charming addition too.

On the whole, the story is intriguing and well-paced. The fae characters are suitably enigmatic and the milieu as fantastic as any lover of fairy tales can ask for, but creating the world of faerie 100% successfully will always be a difficult task. When Catherine and Laon discuss the sea whale, Catherine herself explains the issue:

"It *is* Arcadia," I said. "Who knows what's natural here?"

Readers will bring their own, deeply personal, ideas of what faerie is, (and what it looks like) to the book. Most readers will also understand that faeries are notoriously tricksy, that they can't be trusted and that their behaviour defies logic; hence an author has a tough job to do when writing in the genre – they have to bring consistency to an inconsistent world, and to the events and the various characters' actions, otherwise they won't be able to keep the reader on side, and believing in the unbelievable.

Even Tolkien himself was wary of the work involved in bringing the fae to life through words:

Faërie cannot be caught in a net of words; for it is one of its qualities to be indescribable, though not imperceptible.
—*On Fairy Stories,* J.R.R. Tolkien

On the whole, Ng has managed to keep things consistent, although certain twists of the plot and character actions (the central romance, even) weren't believable. In trying to comprehend the actual mechanics of the pendulum sun (and the implications of how, biologically-speaking, humans would respond physically to such a strange sun) I was puzzled for too long; this wrenched me away from the story.

The core strength of the book is most certainly Ng's attention to detail when it comes to the theology. I appreciated the biblical enigmas presented, and relished Catherine's dialogues with the gardening gnome, Mr Benjamin – a deliciously eccentric yet empathetic character – about what it means to have faith in God.

The book doesn't so much end, as pause, which will, no doubt, irritate some readers, but for those who enjoy spending time in fantastical milieus, the promise of more journeying through Arcadia (and one as evocative and rich as Ng's) will be appreciated.

Carapace
Davyne DeSye
Illuminus, 338 pages
Review by Steve Ironside

Some books you regret picking up, some are just a joy to read, and some feel like a bit of a slog, but at the last page you can put it down and say, "that was worth it". *Carapace* initially felt like it belonged in the first category, but as I continued to read, I came around to fitting it into the last. There's a journey in this novel, and it's worth sticking with it.

The book opens at what feels immediately like the end of part one of the story - painting a picture of a world where humanity has lost. The insectoid aliens (referred to as "ants") have invaded, humanity has been reduced to a slave race on its own planet, and all hope has apparently gone.

The "luckier" humans have been claimed by specific Masters as bodyslaves, who are forced to drink sweetmead, which is then sucked back out of their stomachs, partially digested, for their Master's pleasure. As horrible as this process sounds, being claimed at least protects a human from being summarily executed, or badly treated by other ants. Some Masters take further depraved and more intimate liberties with their slaves, and it is this kind of regular violation that Khara, the first of the characters whose point of view we see, is having to endure.

The book switches viewpoint from chapter to chapter, so we meet the other main characters: Nestra, who is the Shame Accepter for the ant queen (a detoxification process which helps to keep the queen mentally strong), and Samuel, who is a leader for the human Resistance movement while also playing the part of a claimed human. All are undergoing awakenings. As Khara has an epiphany that she can no longer accept what she

CARAPACE
DAVYNE DESYE

SCIENCE FICTION

has become, Nestra begins to see that the queen is insane and that madness is spreading like a sickness. For Samuel, too, there is a growing awareness that defeating the invaders may require more sacrifice than he is prepared for, and that not every rebel may be as they appear at first glance.

The story that DeSye weaves brings these three characters into each other's orbits, set against the final stages of the mad queen's master plan. Will these ordinary rebels succeed in subverting events, or will the queen win, with all that means for both humanity and ant-kind alike?

Initially, I had difficulty getting into the story – the opening chapters are quite short, and the vile, cruel behaviour displayed felt like quite an assault on my sensibilities. I wasn't sure that I wanted to carry on reading if this was all that the book was going to provide. I shouldn't have been concerned – once things settled in, I began to see the point of such a brutal opening.

The emotional flatness of the writing that I'd had such difficulty with had meant that I'd found it hard to empathise and engage with the characters. Then it dawned on me that in an environment where subjugation is the norm, that is what you'd expect. Samuel feels forced to maintain an emotional detachment in order that the work of the resistance is protected, and to ensure that his judgement is unimpaired by attachments. Khara spends much of her time living in a drug-fuelled daze to suppress her reactions to the horrors to which she is subjected daily, and has developed a phobia of being touched by anyone as a result. Nestra is prohibited from touching anyone but the queen, which is often a violent and degrading process, and one which isolates her from the otherwise extremely social nature of her species. The dreary way in which these callous and demeaning acts are described draws you in and has you treating them as normal. Once you are complicit, and acceptant of the way things are, DeSye changes gear, and lets you go through the same awakening as her characters – a neat trick indeed.

And it's once the central characters start to open up to each other, that the emotional palette changes. For some, this is a literal thing. The ants communicate with each other through 'sharing' – a mix of sound, colour, touch and taste – the halting development of trust and communication between Khara, Samuel and Nestra is neatly handled. The description of the extra sensory input when dealing with the ants allows ways of describing the intensity and context of the emotion as a kind of shorthand, like bringing the right music up behind the dialogue in a movie. As a result, the moments where these characters bond feel like they really mean something when compared to the other relationships that exist with the rest of the drone-filled populations, both human and ant. Aside from the emotional content of the book though, there's satisfaction for the intellect too.

Like Brandon Sanderson's excellent *Mistborn* series, this is a book that invites the reader to consider the nature of rebellion, without treating the protagonists as Heroes. What compels an ordinary citizen to act once they are awakened to the injustices that they see around themselves? While both Khara and Nestra do perform heroic acts at times, they aren't heroes in the way that Luke Skywalker is, for example, and while Samuel is lauded for his leadership, he is constantly filled with doubts, but driven to keep doing what he feels is right, rather than being a Hero with a Destiny.

Given the political debates that currently predominate in the media describing disaffected and disenfranchised people being preyed upon by a political elite, led by a distant and volatile leader, there are definite parallels to be drawn if you feel the need to do so. I'm not sure that the book offers any 'quick-fix' solutions, except to demonstrate that trying to effect change requires that individuals act; but it certainly got me thinking about it, which surely is a mark of good sci-fi.

With hints that DeSye has thought ahead to future work in the same universe, I'm intrigued (and to be honest, a little wary) as

to where that could go. Certainly, *Carapace* stands well as a story in its own right, and on that basis, I'd recommend this as a worthwhile read for anyone who likes their sci-fi bleak and gritty, with bit of socio-political allegory to boot.

Off Beat: Nine Spins on Song
Wicked Ink Books, 256 pages
Review by Benjamin Thomas

Off Beat: Nine Spins on Song is a collection of nine lengthy stories that follow inspiration derived from songs that meant something to each writer. Starting with *Basil & Jade* by A.G. Henley and wrapping up with *Thanksgiving in the Park* by R.B. Wood, this collection, while sticking to the theme, is put together in a way that keeps the reader engaged from cover-to-cover.

The potential issue with any themed collection is the possibility of the theme getting stale and redundant by the last story. *Off Beat* avoids this by not only having a solid collection of stories that, while the majority deal with death and spirituality, are original enough that the theme doesn't get old. It also limited the amount of stories to only nine. This helps. While each story is lengthy (approximately 8,000 words) having only nine in the collection prevents the reader from feeling overwhelmed, although the length does make it difficult to read in short bursts.

The collection starts off strong with *Basil & Jade* by A.G. Henley which tackles guilt, love, and suicide. There's a reason the editors led with this story – it's the

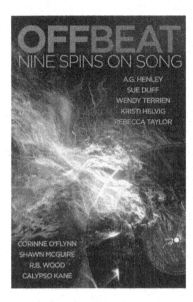

OFFBEAT
NINE SPINS ON SONG

A.G. HENLEY
SUE DUFF
WENDY TERRIEN
KRISTI HELVIG
REBECCA TAYLOR

CORINNE O'FLYNN
SHAWN MCGUIRE
R.B. WOOD
CALYPSO KANE

regarding the song that influenced the story. These snapshot interviews provided in extended depth to the story and, in a few cases, provided new insight into plot and characterization. Each of these were interesting to read, especially for the songs that I already knew. The passages gave credence to the idea that everyone experiences music differently. Each song effecting us in a way that others can't necessarily comprehend.

Walkaway
Cory Doctorow
Head of Zeus, 504 pages
Review by Joanna McLaughlin

What would happen if instead of trying to improve a corrupt society – or even just survive it – we chose to turn our backs on it altogether? This is the premise of Cory Doctorow's new novel, *Walkaway*, in which the main characters decide to abandon 'default' society, and the beliefs on which it's built, to go in search of an alternative being built by other 'walkaways'. While initially ignored by the established state, as increasing numbers of people join the walkaway movement, conflict arises. When a group of walkaways discover a means for people to become immortal, the situation quickly escalates.

Set in a bleak near-future where political and economic power is concentrated in the hands of a small number of privileged families, *Walkaway's* 'default' society feels uncomfortably close to our own world at times. The majority of the population struggle through life, working exploitative, insecure jobs and squatting in

strongest one in the collection. I was instantly hooked on the characters, and while the twist at the end may not have been Earth-shattering it did cause me to raise my eyebrows in slight surprise and appreciation.

My second favorite story in the collection was easily *The Boy Who Wasn't There* by Kristi Helvig. Following two young adults as they attempt to escape a city and the reaches of a crime boss they managed to infuriate, the tension never lets up and the pacing remains consistent throughout the story.

While no story in the collection was weak or unenjoyable, there were a two or three that remained less engaging than others. However, even with a few, subtle weaknesses, the quality of the collection as a whole managed to lift even the unfavorable pieces to a solid height.

At the end of each piece is a brief commentary by the author unsafe accommodation, with little hope of a better life. However, despite its warnings of the devastating impact that hyper-capitalism can have on people and the environment, *Walkaway* is ultimately an optimistic novel; it stresses that this isn't the only future available to us. At the heart of the walkaway movement is the belief that human value isn't derived from lineage, wealth or even their intelligence, but that all people should be valued because they're human beings.

As with most of Doctorow's writings, technology features strongly in *Walkaway*, with 3D printing enabling the walkaways to transform the wreckage of abandoned resources into materials for their new society, creating everything from buildings to food and medicines. The novel also sees a group of talented scientists discover a way to make people live forever, by scanning and storing an online copy of their memories and consciousness. However, it's not technology but ideology that takes centre stage, with a significant amount of the novel dedicated to exploring complex questions about what's truly important in life and what we're willing to do to hold onto those things.

At 504 pages the novel feels a little long, with a significant amount of time dedicated to hearing the main characters voicing different view-points about how society could and should work. Whilst some of the scenes feel a little unnecessary and slow down the plot, they never feel unrealistic. Indeed, instead of battling an 'evil

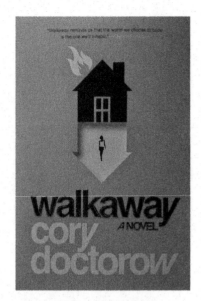

villain' it's refreshing that much of the conflict in the novel arises from the walkaways struggling to unite over a shared vision of their ideal society.

The early stages of the novel also feel a little inaccessible at times, and it is initially a struggle to become immersed in the story. However, by calling his main character Hubert Vernon Rudolph Clayton Irving Wilson Alva Anton Jeff Harley Timothy Curtis Cleveland Cecil Ollie Edmund Eli Wily Marvin Ellis Espinoza (or Hubert, etc. for short) it's difficult not to think that this complexity was Doctorow's intention and in the same way that the reader might struggle to connect with the default world, so do the characters we follow.

Despite these niggles, *Walkaway* is an exciting, thought-provoking read that any Cory Doctorow fan is sure to enjoy. This one certainly did!

The Delirium Brief
Charles Stross
Orbit, 435 pages

Review by Duncan Lunan

The press release for this novel begins "James Bond meets H.P. Lovecraft in the latest occult thriller from Hugo Award winner Charles Stross, in a series where British spies take on the supernatural". The Bond reference is apt because it's sometimes alleged that the 00-numbers go back to Elizabethan times, possibly to Francis Walsingham's agents, signifying either 'the eyes of the Queen' or 'For Your Eyes Only' in coded messages to her. And the real-life connections of Ian Fleming and his brother Peter to the wartime Special Operations Executive are well known, although neither was directly involved in it.

In this novel and its predecessors, the SOE, aka 'The Laundry', genuinely goes back to Elizabethan times (probably involving John Dee, though not mentioned here) and has been kept secret since, because its principal brief has been to protect Britain from harmful supernatural forces. Its cover has been blown by a major incursion of elves which has been contained, but involved severe damage and loss of life in south Yorkshire. A government looking for scapegoats and hell-bent (as it were) on privatisation, particulary handing over national assets to US corporations, has swept the SOE aside with no idea of the multiple problems that will unleash, and still less awareness that the outwardly Christian US organisation, so keen to take over, is actually a front for trans-dimensional beings with similarities to things in H.P. Lovecraft, *Star Trek: Wrath of Khan*, and various invasive nasties from *Dr. Who* and *Babylon 5*. In our world, the parallels with Brexit and TTIP are too obvious to need emphasis.

Recently I reviewed *Into the Guns* by William S. Dietz for the Shoreline of Infinity website, drawing a comparison with Nevil Shute's *In the Wet* and suggesting that the British Armed Forces' oath of loyalty to the Queen might prevent fragmentation in crisis, like the US military one which Dietz portrays. The comparison is appropriate here too, because the executives and operatives of the Laundry are similarly motivated – though it seems to be an abstract loyalty to 'the Crown', whose precise definition is debated, rather than to the sovereign in person. There are some intriguing references to a little-known Act of Parliament giving the heir to the throne authority to use nuclear weapons – something which the

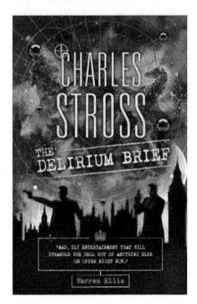

Laundry has been careful to keep secret from the current holder of the title. I did wonder if it would provide a Final Solution for surviving units of the Yorkshire invasion, only temporarily held in check, but if Stross has that in mind it must be for a later book.

There's also a parallel with the mediaeval organisation of the Knights Templar, with the Masters corresponding to the SOE executives and the Knights to the secret agents. The Templar Knights and Masters were comparatively few in number, and were supported by a much larger force of sergeants and other staff who ran the vast network of farms, ships, etc, needed to maintain the force in the Holy Land. Similarly the Laundry's operations in the UK and beyond are staffed by a great many workers who are simply given their P.45s and told to report to the DSS in the morning. We don't see much of the resulting chaos, but what we do see is that lack if manpower forces the upper echelons of the Laundry to make deals with people and powers whom they've hitherto imprisoned or suppressed. In fighting the greater evil, former enemies have to become friends or at least uneasy allies. I was reminded of Churchill's comment, on reversing his attitude to Stalin when Hitler invaded Russia: "If Hitler invaded hell, I would make at least a favourable reference to the Devil in the House of Commons." (I first heard it as 'to His Satanic Majesty', which seems even better.) Still, up till then I was mentally congratulating Stross on making the novel accessible to a new reader of the series. The stand-alone aspect was seriously weakened in the later sections as more and more people and beings from previous novels were released from captivity to join the conflict; and some parts of the victory seemed to come too easily, relying too much on thriller and fantasy tropes – e.g. that a trained operative, or a novice, has only to slip into a waitress costume to become invisible and penetrate the household of a security-conscious enemy.

Anyway, we are left at the end with a fox in charge of the henhouse on this side of the Atlantic, and the alien takeover unopposed on the other. As R.M. Freeman wrote at the outbreak of World War 2, when his *Saml. Pepys and the Minxes* column was axed by *The Listener*: "What will come of it all, God knows." But no doubt Charles Stross will be back to tell us, and we have that to look forward to.

Multiverse

Russell Jones

Welcome to the MultiVerse! This time we've something a little different: three poets, plus a piece of artwork from renowned comics artist Sydney Jordan. The art was produced to accompany Marise Morland's poem, "Press Conference", which begins our poetic journey in this issue…

"Press Conference" introduces us to a "girl who scandalised two worlds" for jilting a "Nibiru lord". As she describes his arrogance and their rocky relationship, we realise the speaker far outweighs her famous husband in panache, intellect and bite. Morland's second poem, "Peturbations", deals with a broken relationship (although whether it's with a human, another species or a planetary body is another question), coming to the realisation that we each learn to move on, that "it wasn't much; / the skies didn't fall".

Bill Herbert's "Google Mars" explores photos of the red planet, and considers how distant images might remind us of the past. We fill in the gaps created by a photo's "checkered veil" until scenes are "rendered ever more earthly / / local". The present, past and future blend into one, and personal memories are transposed onto alien landscapes.

In "L5" by Peter Roberts, we're told that life can seem artificial "like an airport terminal" – an existence which we shuffle through almost mechanically. However, the poem shifts, searching the "stars, earth, & moon", trying to find a place of belonging. This disjoint encourages us to think about our consciousness and our place in the universe: are we drifting through life mindlessly, or searching for something greater? Roberts' second poem, "the evening after", paints a near-apocalyptic ("broken mushroom cloud") scene of the moon rising over its "new-made / twin landscape". It probes the self-destructive tendencies of humanity, whilst highlighting the perseverance and indifference of physics and the natural worlds.

Press Conference

I need no introduction, gentlemen.
I'm the girl who scandalised two worlds,
the minx who jilted a Nibiru lord.
What? Am I ashamed? Why should I be?
Oh yes, I've heard the gossip. Didn't know
which side her bread was buttered, and so on.
Of course I was surprised when he chose me.
He could have had his pick of the elite.
And what was I? A mere translator. No,
it wasn't the publicity that scared me.
I knew what to expect. The constant bitching,
from "what does he see in her" to "what will she find
under his robes?" Boys, let me be frank.
That wasn't the problem. Nor was it the rant
from my future mother-in-law. In time
I learnt to sparkle at the state occasions
and endless presentations. Just as well
his mother specified a long engagement;
it all came true, her snide predictions
that he'd still drink and party with his pals,
that he'd dictate what I should wear and eat.
I learnt tolerance. He was young and spoilt.
But one thing rankled always. This will sound
so trivial: he walked ahead of me.
Marginalised, ignored, too many times
I watched his arrogant complacent back -
purple cloak resplendently aswirl -
and willed him desperately to turn around.
And once, I said "I'm not Eurydice."
He didn't get it. Greek mythology
wasn't on the cultural manifest.
So, I left. And yes, I've often wondered
how long he took to realise. Well, that's it.
Interview over. Now, which polite young man
murmured "after you" as we came in?
I'll grant you an additional exclusive.
Please wait. The rest of you may go.

Marise Morland

Perturbations

They told me you'd be back,
creating havoc, dishing out
unasked-for advice.
I made arrangements, vowing I'd
defy your overweening presence,
try to protect my trusting brood
from heeding your false promises
and gravitating to you.

We paused, circled one another.
You made a move.
I countered it, felt
the pull of old attractions
threaten my long-established balance.

And then the event was past.
In cosmic terms it wasn't much;
the skies didn't fall
and if someone somewhere
detected a starquake,
it was a very small one.

We meet, we separate,
the cycle starts anew
on the ground bass of our lives.

Marise Morland

Marise Morland-Chapman is a native of High Wycombe, and has had short SF
and fantasy stories published since the 1980's in magazines including *Practical
Computing, Beyond, Auguries* and *Scheherazade*. Her poetry has been in many
periodicals and won 3 regional awards including a commendation from the Yeats
Society. In 1988 she collaborated with Sydney Jordan on the comic strip "Time
and Ms. Jones" which was published in the Funday section of the Sunday Times,
and reprinted in Italy last year. For the past few years she has been working on a
quartet of space opera novels.

Sydney Jordan (born Dundee, Scotland, 1928) is a comics artist best known for his
daily science fiction strip Jeff Hawke, which ran in the Daily Express from 1955 to
1974. After Jeff Hawke finished, Jordan created another science fiction strip, Lance
McLane, which ran in the Scottish newspaper the Daily Record from 1976 to
1988. In the mid seventies Sydney produced the one shot Hall Star for the Dutch
comic strip weekly Eppo, which he didn't complete until the mid eighties.

Google Mars

Its first images now are like the old moon
landings' static tapestry, that checkered veil
through which we still see footprint, visor, flag;
or the way the dead recede or retreat while
remaining in the corner of your eye, ear, thought.

Knowing they will always be renewed -
the streamless creeks and lizardless rocks
we roam down and past, zooming and dragging
the viewer eagerly from gulch to wasteland;
their same scenes rendered ever more earthly,

local in that way the unwashed looks familiar -
grants the pixelation upgradable nostalgia,
like that footage of the first dog, the one
that could never come back: how it ran, red tongue
lolling, the poly-tunnel's length as though

down the side of an as-yet unbuilt house,
and we all knew one day we'd be at home.

Bill Herbert

Bill Herbert is mostly published by Bloodaxe Books. Recent volumes include
Omnesia and, with Donut Press, ***Murder Bear*** (both 2013). He is Professor of
Poetry and Creative Writing at Newcastle University, and Dundee's Makar, or
City Laureate. In 2014 he won a Cholmondeley Award, and in 2015 was made a
Fellow of the Royal Literary Society.

L5

2

it's life in a shopping mall, all
the time. everything expensive;
harsh light – harsher air.
like an airport terminal,
alien & alienating, &
behind smooth surfaces
strange, subtle machines
at the center, heart & meaning,
keep the functioning smooth –
& people seem superfluous.

3

& yet, looking out
at stars, earth, & moon
(the stars, too, seem small
in the great all-in-all),
we seem to fit in; our
personal nothingness
seamlessly shades
into global non-being;
our vacuity fills
the universe-vacuum.
comfortably hollow,
we feel nothing, so we feel
we belong, after all.

Peter Roberts

the evening after

half-dissipated, broken mushroom cloud
curls around the full moon
– black scorpion tail, edged in silver,
ready to strike. too late now, poison
already spent, the unnatural beast
lets the moon go. the moon rises higher,
stands out above dying clouds, shines
a cold light over its new-made
twin landscape: barren, crater–riddled,
rubble & dust surface.

wind barely bothers the
fine-structure powder;
only the clouds
& moon truly move.

Peter Roberts

Peter Roberts is a mathematically educated poet who sometimes writes fiction. He has been contributing to various magazines and journals for more than 40 years. See his slightly out-of-date personal webpage, www.god-and-country. info/personal.html, where you can find links to lists of all his published poems & stories, if you look carefully enough. Some may find the rest of the website interesting as well.

Parabolic Puzzles
Paul Holmes

The Asteroid Belt

We were growing weary and it was time to grab a bite to eat and retire before our busy day planned for tomorrow. The Conference Centre was expected to be packed with visitors and delegations from all of the planets in the Federation, with talks ranging from the latest in warp drive technology (Matt would have undoubtedly booked a seat for this) to legal aspects of ownership of wormholes (Josh was an interstellar property lawyer), and with concerts as diverse as the Sirian Philharmonic to a Yorkshire Brass Band (that was Ricardus' morning sorted).

The four pals left the Bud-Eyed Monster and walked across town to the Asteroid Belt, a glorified burger joint with exotic waitresses and flaming cocktails. Well—we were on holiday after all.

After a sumptuous meal of Altarian Angus burgers, French fries and Sonic Screwdrivers, we decided to split the bill equally four ways. The bill came to Ł374.00 (Ł = Logonian dollars) and so we all placed a Ł100 note on the tray (credit transactions were very expensive away from one's home planet) and told our waitress to keep the change.

"Thank you, gentlemen, but tipping is illegal on Logon Alpha. I shall get you your change."

Back at the till the waitress realised that she had overcharged massively for the drinks and the total should have been Ł321. It had been a busy night and the restaurant was out of small denominations so instead of returning the full amount (figuring, quite reasonably, that we would be happy with more change than expected), she gave us each a Ł10 note, kept Ł 39 for herself and bid us a pleasant evening.

We left the Asteroid Belt and retired to our various rooms, promising to meet up at the Conference Centre in the morning.

But we paid Ł360 and she kept Ł39 making Ł399. The question was—what had happened to the missing Logonian Dollar?

HOW TO SUPPORT SCOTLAND'S SCIENCE FICTION MAGAZINE

CONER '17

BECOME A PATRON

SHORELINE OF INFINITY HAS A *PATREON* PAGE AT

WWW.PATREON.COM/ SHORELINEOFINFINITY

ON *PATREON*, YOU CAN PLEDGE A MONTHLY PAYMENT FROM AS *LOW AS $1* IN EXCHANGE FOR A *COOL TITLE* AND A *REGULAR REWARD*.

ALL PATRONS GET AN *EARLY DIGITAL ISSUE* OF THE MAGAZINE QUARTERLY AND *EXCLUSIVE ACCESS* TO OUR PATREON MESSAGE FEED AND SOME GET *A LOT MORE*. HOW ABOUT THESE?

POTENT PROTECTOR SPONSORS A STORY EVERY YEAR WITH FULL CREDIT IN THE MAGAZINE WHILE AN *AWESOME AEGIS* SPONSORS AN ILLUSTRATION.

TRUE BELIEVER SPONSORS A *BEACHCOMBER COMIC* AND *MIGHTY MENTOR* SPONSORS A COVER PICTURE.

AND .... OUR HIGHEST HONOUR ... *SUPREME SENTINEL* SPONSORS A *WHOLE ISSUE* OF SHORELINE OF INFINITY.

ASK *YOUR FAVOURITE BOOK SHOP* TO GET YOU A COPY. WE ARE ON THE *TRADE DISTRIBUTION LISTS*.

OR BUY A COPY *DIRECTLY* FROM OUR *ONLINE SHOP* AT

WWW.SHORELINEOFINFINITY.COM

YOU CAN GET AN *ANNUAL SUBSCRIPTION* THERE TOO.

KINDLE FANS CAN GET SHORELINE FROM THE *AMAZON KINDLE STORE*.

Lightning Source UK Ltd.
Milton Keynes UK
UKOW06f1649120917
309065UK00006B/81/P